Nanni Balestrini

We Want Everything

the novel of Italy's hot autumn

Translated by Matt Holden

VERSO

London • New York

First published in this Verso edition 2016
Translation © Matt Holden 2014, 2016
Introduction © Rachel Kushner 2016

First published in English by Telephone Publishing, Melbourne, 2014
First published as *Vogliamo tutto* © Giangiacomo Feltrinelli Editori, Milan, 1971

1 3 5 7 9 10 8 6 4 2

Verso
UK: 6 Meard Street, London W1F 0EG
US: 20 Jay Street, Suite 1010, Brooklyn, NY 11201
versobooks.com

Verso is the imprint of New Left Books

ISBN-13: 978-1-78478-368-6
ISBN-13: 978-1-78478-371-6 (US EBK)
ISBN-13: 978-1-78478-370-9 (UK EBK)

British Library Cataloguing in Publication Data
A catalogue record for this book is available from the British Library

Library of Congress Cataloging-in-Publication Data
A catalog record for this book is available from the Library of Congress

Book design by Warren Taylor (Monash Art, Design & Architecture)
Typeset in Caponi
Printed in the US by Maple Press

To Alfonso

Contents

In the penultimate moment of Luchino Visconti's 1960 film *Rocco and His Brothers*, the factory siren of an Alfa Romeo plant on the outskirts of Milan sounds, indicating that it's time for Ciro, one of Rocco's brothers, to return to work. The workers, Ciro among them, all turn around and head toward the gates, showing viewers the famous automotive logo on the back of their coveralls. Ciro is the 'good' brother, the one who found a way to live in industrial northern Italy: he accepts his social position as an unskilled worker, marries a nice local petty bourgeois girl, and lives cleanly. Ciro has just reported his brother Simone to the police. Simone has murdered Nadia, a prostitute he and Rocco have fought over. Rocco has gone off to pursue a career in the brutal world of professional boxing. The family is shattered and dispersed. The youngest brother, Luca, standing outside the Alfa plant with Ciro, says he hopes to someday return to the southern region of Lucania, where they're from.

Why would they have left Lucania to begin with, a world where you relax in the sun, go to the beach, take a tomato from the vine when you're hungry? There was chronic underemployment in the south. The soil was of poor quality. After grain markets were deregulated, prices plummeted. For rural populations in the Mezzogiorno there was simply no future. At the same time, the Italian postwar economic 'miracle' meant there were jobs in the factories of the rapidly industrialising north. Between 1951 and 1971, 9 million people migrated from rural to industrial areas in Italy. They often arrived in the big cities with nothing, and were forced to live in train station waiting rooms or on relatives' floors, if they had that option. They worked day and evening shifts on building sites or in factories that offered treacherous conditions and long hours.

This history is all deftly evoked in Visconti's film: the alienation that Rocco's family finds in damp and cold Milan, an abject and miserable life in the basement of a housing project, and their attempts to survive in a city where they are little more than pariahs, *terroni* excluded from northern working-class life. The film ends after the southerners return from lunch to their shift on the assembly lines at Alfa Romeo, and yet the saga is not over. It is far from over. The end of the film opens outward to the portents of the future. To what was to come, and eventually did come.

Almost a decade later, in 1969, the workers from the south on the assembly lines of the north revolted in waves of wildcat strikes and violence. And yet it was not really a *workers'* movement along the available spectrum, then, of worker organisations and, most notably, the Communist Party. May Day, for instance, a celebration of work, seemed imbecilic to these newly migrated workers in revolt. They regarded the Communist Party as an impediment to real change and little more, an organ of compromise with company bosses. These workers were ready to reject the entire structure of northern life and of work itself. Their revolt was an all-out assault on their own exploitation. They wanted everything, as their placard slogan and shop floor chant famously expressed, *Vogliamo Tutto!*

We Want Everything is a novel of great energy and originality that succeeds on three different levels simultaneously, as a work of astounding art, a document of history, and a political analysis that remains resonant to the contradictions of the present. The artfulness lies in the tone: the person who speaks in the first person in this novel is nameless, but not at all unknown to us. He is intimate, insolent, blunt. He's full of personality, full of humour, and rage. He speaks in a kind of vernacular poetry that gets into the mind, and stays there. 'All this new stuff in the city had a price on it,' he says, 'from the newspaper to the meat to the shoes; everything had a price.' His story is likely that of a real person, named Alfonso Natella, to whom the book is dedicated. Perhaps crucially, the protagonist speaks in a vaguely testimonial form to those who were not there. He was there, and he knows we, his readers, were not, and so he gives us a full account of his life. The book in its entire first half is something like a dossier, and we know the dossier matters: it's the case file of someone who was witness to the clashes and convulsions of his own historical era.

Our hero arrives in Turin and is lucky enough to have a place to sleep at his sister's, while many of the 'great tide' of southerners washing into Turin are living in the second-class waiting room at Porta Nuova train station, which would admit anyone with a Fiat ID card or a letter from Fiat stating that he had an interview at the factory. The police patrolled the train station vigilantly, but not on the lookout for loiterers and squatters. The police were looking for journalists, making sure they didn't get anywhere near the second-class waiting room, 'this dormitory, for free, that Fiat had at the Torino train station', as the protagonist says.

At the Fiat plant, he seeks employment along with 20,000 other new hires. 'The monsters were coming,' he says, 'the horrible workers.' And their monstrosity is magnified by the high demand for labour. Many workers left after just a few days, the work was so unbearable. Some withstood only half a day before choosing destitution over the demands of the assembly line. The protagonist is part of this tide of necessary monsters, hated that much more because the factory must hire them, must deal with them.

He goes through an interview process that is a pantomime (everyone is hired), then a factory medical assessment, which is even more comical and absurd. The protagonist endures muscle-strength testing on newfangled machinery, a blood test in a room that features high piles of stinking, blood-soaked cotton balls, a piss test that the men prepare for in a circle, 'making beer', as they joke, and then finally, the doctor's examination, in which the protagonist, for the hell of it, seeing that the whole thing is a charade, announces that he is missing one testicle.

He's hired despite his lie. They are all hired. 'Maybe they wouldn't have taken a paraplegic', the protagonist speculates. But the medical exam has not been *entirely* a charade. To this reader it seems a necessary stage in these workers' exploitation: they are handing over the rights to their sole possession—their bodies—to the bosses of Fiat, transferring ownership of their selves to the factory. And so when the protagonist claims to the company doctor that he's only got one ball, he is throwing *them* an insult, telling them that their new body on the line is faulty; it's not even a full man!

On the assembly line, the real fun begins. The work is back-breaking, and in this era, wages were tied to productivity, meaning workers didn't get a decent base wage; they could not earn enough to live on unless they produced a certain profit margin for the company. At one point our protagonist is put on a line where the work requires use of just one shoulder to rivet with a heavy pneumatic gun, a repeated motion that will deform him by twisting his back and bulking his muscles asymmetrically. Meanwhile there are some on the assembly line who are dedicated to work and to the Communist Party (PCI), northerners from peasant backgrounds, 'really hard people, a bit dense, lacking in imagination', who spend their whole short lives working. People for whom 'work was everything'. To the narrator, they're worthless. 'Only a drone', he says, 'could spend years in this shitty prison and do a job that destroys your life.'

Most of the new workers are like the protagonist—alien to the prison of the factory, and they can't stand the conditions. They fill the infirmaries with fake and real injuries until it looks like a field hospital. The protagonist hurts his finger, but only a little. He puts some black grease on it and asks for time off. When the doctor touches it, our hero swears in dialect. 'If I swore in Italian', he says, 'it would seem like I was acting, but swearing in Neapolitan, the guy didn't know if I was acting or not. Mannaggia 'a maronna, me stai cacando 'o cazzo, statte fermo porco dio, that kind of thing.' Everyone is acting. The protagonist is acting the part of the *terrone*, and the doctor is playing the role of factory authority who, wearily, doesn't much care.

The protagonist gets sick leave, but realises that he has no idea what to do with himself, how to relax or what to do in Turin. The factory not only degrades work, it degrades the life away from work, too. This is alienation, the lived experience of exploitation, but it is demonstrated here without theoretical abstractions: it's an oral account of a person's life, that's all.

At a turning point, the narrator decides to dedicate himself totally to making trouble. It's a commitment to risk everything. 'I didn't want Fiat,' he tells the bosses. 'I didn't make it. I'm inside here just to make money and that's it. But if you piss me off and break my balls I'll smash your heads in, all of you.'

And so the struggle begins. But the protagonist's threat, that scene, is not a moment of singular heroism. As literature and history both, *We Want Everything* is not a story of one remarkable man. It's the story of the nameless and unknown who went north, like Rocco and his brothers and like the 20,000 who were hired the month the protagonist was hired, in 1969. It's the story of the men who worked these awful jobs and got fed up, directed their rage and their strength and violence, in the interest of no longer living in misery. (The women would not have their say quite yet: this struggle was about men and their exploitation, while women—exploited doubly in Italy, in the piece work they did at kitchen tables for the factories in the north, and by their families, for their domestic labour, domestic toil—would have to mark out their own path, and did. In fact it's accurate to say that feminism had the most lasting and successful impact among the demands made in the revolts of 1970s Italy. But women's demands were not part of the 'everything' in this everything of factory revolts, a reminder that the word has limits, a context. 'We want everything' meant we want to live lives with meaning, and we refuse to be forced to work in order to survive. It was a working-class male 'everything'; women would still be at home toiling away, even in the case of unlikely victory.)

The second part of the novel opens with a chapter on the wage, and marks the narrator's transformation into a theorist of his own struggle. He sees that as a worker whose wages are tied to productivity, he collaborates with the bosses against himself. The tone makes a subtle shift. The 'I' partly dissolves, and the book becomes something like pirate radio news bulletins of the war on the factory, the war in the streets. The struggle expands. The narrator, wherever he is now, is part of a new collective desire, calling not for higher base pay but the abolition of capitalism, for the bosses' economy to collapse.

I once asked a friend, an Italian from Milan who seems to know a lot of people, if he'd heard of Nanni Balestrini. My friend is in the art world, and I wasn't sure if he would have read Balestrini's work. We were in this friend's kitchen. He was making me a salad. He said 'Balestrini!? Nanni? But I helped him escape into France!' It turned out that, in 1979, when Nanni was going to be arrested as so many were, for so-called insurrectionary activities against the state, this friend outfitted Balestrini with skis and ski gear. Drove him to the Italian Alps, and then crossed into France and waited for Balestrini to ski down on the other side of Mont Blanc, into Chamonix. I pictured the one photo I'd seen of Balestrini, a man wearing a scarf wrapped in a complicated and elegant manner, a person who looked more bohemian and urbane than athletic. I asked, 'But does Balestrini *ski*?' My friend held out his hands in emphasis, and said, 'You know ... good enough!'

Balestrini had been a founding member, in 1968, of the extra-parliamentary left-wing group Potere Operaio, whose focus was on factories and factory workers, on listening to workers and producing a movement of their voices and direct experience. It's likely Balestrini was outside the gates of Fiat in 1969. (Alfonso Natella, the subject and 'ghost author' of this novel was also involved with Potere Operaio, which is surely how they met.) This method of workers' inquiry—called *inchiesta* by its practitioners in Italy—has foundations in Marxism, but only truly took hold in postwar Europe, particularly in the tactics and tenets of the radical left French group Socialism or Barbarism, which then influenced workerist theory—*Operaismo*—in Italy. Worker subjectivity, it became apparent, was shifting, from building a labour movement to a resistance against the disciplines of work. The concept of collecting the stories of workers themselves, the idea that their accounts of work and of their lives would be essential to any revolutionary process, goes all the way back to Marx's 1880 worker's questionnaire, which was meant to be disseminated among French factory workers. 'It is the workers in town and country', Marx wrote, 'who alone can describe with full knowledge the misfortunes from which they suffer.' Simply put, there is no theory without struggle. Struggle is the conditions of possibility for theory. And struggle is produced by workers themselves.

But in its utilisation by Balestrini, who was not just a militant and theorist but a poet and artist, a writer to the core, inchiesta became something more, something else: a singular artistic achievement and a new literary form, the novel–inchiesta. Balestrini went on to employ this same method in later novels, *Gli Invisibli* (*The Unseen*), and *Sandokan*, both of which feature first-person protagonists who tell stories that serve also as historical accounts, the militancy of the autonomist movement of 1977, and the Camorra and its ravages of the south, respectively. These voices in Balestrini's novels are always one person speaking anonymously as a type. The voices have all the specificity of an individual—a set of attitudes, moods, prejudices, back stories, but they each speak in a way that exemplifies what life was like *for a person such as them*, in a moment when there were many like them. They are works that capture and illuminate voice. Voices speaking, rather than words written. In this way, these works depart from the classical subjectivity of the nineteenth-century novel, and seem closer in relation to an earlier tradition, also oral, and heroic, and historic: epic poetry.

We need many epics for each epoch. If only we had the testimony of Balestrini's own life, his own *I* as an *any* and a *we*, his militancy and flight. In the creation of *We Want Everything*, he dissolved himself, became the mere medium through which Alfonso Natella speaks. As if Balestrini had rolled under the factory gates, like smoke, and was suddenly inside. Perhaps the novel–inchiesta is never a work of introspection, but always instead of refraction: a way to refract that which, as Umberto Eco wrote of this novel, "is already literature" *before* its refraction, its transcription, before its existence in a book.

This novel was already literature when it was in the form of the passing thoughts a worker was having on the assembly line. And yet I'd like to think that Balestrini skiing down into Chamonix, his scarf flapping, whether told or not, is literature, too.

più uma
SCIOP
Fiat: la l.
FIAT: rilancio dell
Il comunismo
POTERE
dell organizzazion
STRUIRE L'ORGANIZ
ONE RIVO DALLA FABBRI
ZIONARIA A ALLA SCUOL
AL TERRITORI
LLA CRISI LOTTA DURA
OTERE DEL CAPITAL

a **O** del lavoro?

RO FIAT: RIUSCITO

"male oscuro dell'economia

tta la classe opera

lotta del **HA DETTO**

OPERAIO

Costruiamo l'offensiva sul
fruttamento capitalistico tigre
ruttamento capitalistico di
Sfruttamento capitalistico cart
ttamento capitalistico
la reazione degli operai

al cuore
a colpit

tolto con la violenza
alla classe operaia

previous pages: Nanni Balestrini *Potere operaio*, collage, 1972

First part

First chapter **The south**

In the south it had already been 10 or 15 years since it started. The intervention of the Cassa,[1] the new industries, the countryside that had to be industrialised. And at all the rallies you went to they said for progress in the south you had to work. For a new human dignity you had to produce. That you needed a new south, development, bread for everyone, work for everyone and all that. The Christian Democrats said it, the Communist Party said it, they all said it.

Instead it was the green light for emigration, the signal for everyone to go to the factories up north. Because in northern Italy and Europe the factories were ready to take that mass of people. The assembly lines at Volkswagen and Fiat needed them all. And that was the type of worker they needed: a worker who could do any job on the line, who had been a labourer or a road digger in the south and who could, when necessary, just as easily be unemployed.

Before it had been the other way around. Labourers had to stay peasants, they had to stay tied to the land. The workers of the south had to all stay tied to the south. Because if they'd all gone to work in the north and in Europe before about 15 years ago there would have been a big mess up there. Because they weren't ready with all the factories and everything up there then. I didn't know about these things that had happened, before. I learned about them by talking to the comrades. After I'd given up on work, for good. After the trouble I started that day at Mirafiori.[2]

At that time in the south the Communist Party's slogan was: Land to whoever works. But what the hell did a labourer care about the land, about owning the land. They only thing he cared about was the money that he didn't have: the security of having it guaranteed, all year round. In the end the Communist Party in the south changed its policies from the time of the land occupations. It retreated into the provincial towns, where there was nothing to do except run along behind dissatisfied tradesmen and office workers. Meanwhile the big struggles at Battipaglia[3] and Reggio[4] exploded, though the Communist Party thought those people were just a shitty underclass.

Apart from anything else, it's not as if the south in general had ever been poor. The landowners had always made plenty of money, and that continued after the Cassa del Mezzogiorno, except it was only the big landowners who kept making money, while anyone with less than five hectares was supposed to just disappear.

4

Take, for example, the owners of the fertile land on the outskirts of Salerno on the Sele plain. There were *pommaroli* on the plain, people who plant tomatoes every season, with the whole family working. Little by little, as they made some money, the landowners turned all this work into an industry. Now they do it all, from field to can. And the labourers become workers, and with machines there are fewer people working but they're producing more. And the other people from around there, well, they're meant to just disappear.

The rich landowners whose land was expropriated by the Cassa pocketed hundreds of millions of lire. It was in their interest, too, to see industry develop. With all those millions they built apartments in the cities, thousands of them. The people who came to work on the building sites weren't from Salerno, most came from out of town: from the interior, from villages in the mountains, from the Apennines. They were all people who owned a house, a pig, some chickens, some vines, olives, oil, but who could no longer get by. They sold up, bought apartments in the city, got jobs in the factories. And so the unemployed in the cities stayed unemployed; in fact, there were more than before.

It was especially the people from the interior and the villages in the Apennines who had to go up north. The Cassa did nothing for them, it was as if they were supposed to just disappear. Go north for development, because our underdevelopment was useful to them in the north, it helped their development. Who developed the north, who developed all of Italy and Europe? We did, the labourers of the south. It was as if northern workers and southern labourers were something different, something other than an underclass. It's us, southerners, who are the workers of the north. What is Torino if it's not a southern city? Who works there? Just like Salerno, like Reggio, like Battipaglia. Corso Traiano happened, the same as Battipaglia, when people realised that they couldn't go on. All the stories of work up there and down here, there is work or there isn't work, it's a scam. You understand that the only answer is to burn everything, like at Battipaglia. The same thing will happen everywhere soon when we get organised. And in the end we'll change everything. We'll tell them all to get fucked, them and their shitty jobs.

The building workers came to Salerno from Nocera, Cava, San Cipriano Picentino, Giffoni, Montecorvino. They came from all these towns in the morning on scooters and mopeds. There was a lot of work building factories, truck drivers to carry cement, stone, steel, to make roads and everything. There was a building boom in Salerno in the '50s. Everyone bought scooters or mopeds. You saw the first mass-market car, the 600, which even workers had. And everyone bought TVs, antennas sprouted all over the place.

Money really started to circulate. And there was always more stuff in the clothing shops and the grocers, and new shops were opening all the time. Everyone made more and spent more in Salerno. But generally it wasn't the working class or the unemployed from Salerno. It was the people from the villages around. Money got to those villages, but naturally it didn't stay there. You busted your arse every day to come on your moped or scooter or in your 600 from Montecorvino to Salerno for work, and then turned around and went back every evening. Then you looked for an apartment in town. In fact, all the new apartments in Salerno housed people who had come from out of town.

Lots of people worked on the building sites and then lived in the apartments they'd built. After a while they went to live in these apartments in town, renting and even buying them. These people weren't proletarians like in the city, the people who had fuck-all. In their own way they were land owners, they had the house, the pig, chickens, grape vines, olive trees and olive oil. And they also managed to buy apartments in town. Then they found jobs in the factories. To be taken on in a factory, you needed a raccomandazione.[5] These yokels brought prosciutto to their local councillors. They brought oil, wine, all kinds of stuff and that's how they got jobs. That was the only way they managed to find a position. And then they became proletarians like those in town, although that's really what they had been all along.

I found a job through an uncle, too. Now he's retired; he worked in the finanza. He had a cousin in the employment office. He took me to the employment office and said to his cousin: this is one of my nephews. You have to help him, you have to find him a job somewhere. He gave me some paperwork, sent me along to Ideal Standard. I had an interview, passed the health insurance medical. Then I went back for the aptitude test. You did the aptitude test at the same time as the office workers. But we had longer. They had to do it in a minute, we had three. Then they said they were sending us to do a course. The guys who'd done best in the aptitude test went to do a course in Brescia.

We asked why we were going to do this course. They said the Cassa was paying for training to get southern technicians ready for southern industry. When I heard talk about a course I thought it was just a technical thing. The whole time I was unemployed after I finished technical school I did courses. Works mechanic, fitter and turner, I did courses in all these things but I learnt fuck-all: they were no use at all. They were only there so the employment office looked like it was training people. I don't know what the political motives behind the schools were.

Anyway, when I heard course I thought we were going there to listen and have things explained to us. They gave us tickets to Brescia and lunch for the journey. At Brescia station a social worker from Ideal Standard was waiting for us. They called taxis and they knew us by name, all twenty of us. Ten here, five there, seven somewhere else: they'd even found pensiones for us to stay in. These are the pensione we've found, they said. If you don't like them you can move. And the next day we turned up at Ideal Standard. They told us we were good lads, strong and all of that, and they ask us if we'd like to go to France or Torino or Milano. The company ran regular excursions. But we really didn't give a stuff about the excursions, so we said, yeah, sure, OK.

They gave us white overalls with the IS logo on them. They took us into the factory, where the temperature was in the 30s. It was humid because of all the ceramics drying: the water evaporates and everything gets soaked. We felt like we were suffocating. We had darker skin than the Ideal Standard workers from Brescia. Being in that heat and humidity all the time you have to shower every night, and your skin gets paler. And it's not as if there's much sun in Brescia. Coming from the south, where it was the end of summer, we were black, which scared them all a little.

Anyway, they show us the toilet bowls, the bidets, the hand basins, the stands for the hand basins, the bathtubs. They show us cross-sections, explain how thick they have to be. How many minutes a hand basin has to stay in the mould, how many minutes all the different pieces have to stay in the mould. They explain how the mould is made and other stuff. And then they start to show us how you do it. I could see that the workers from Brescia did the work straight out without thinking about it too much, bam, bam, just like that, almost like it was nothing. So I said to myself, Christ, what the fuck is this course about? Are we talking about real work here, or about becoming foremen?

All right, I thought, if we're talking about becoming foremen then we won't have to work much, and so I took it easy. My workmates worked on two toilets while I made one, and I went along like that. After we'd been there two or three months we joined this struggle. There were strikes, and we went on strike too, instinctively, with the guys from Brescia. The Cassa del Mezzogiorno paid us; we got ten thousand lire a week living allowance, more than forty thousand a month. And they paid us sixty thousand lire a month and we had free meals, in the company canteen. We had free transport all over the city, on every route.

Before Brescia every one of us was from a different town, from different areas. We all lived the typical southern life. But there five or six of us stayed at each pensione, we ate together, we caught the bus together, and so we started to understand the advantages of industrial work. It wasn't as if they were exploiting us in that work, we were only being trained. We didn't feel exploited, at least, that was our impression. Some union organisers from the factory came to see us, saying that once we went back down south we'd have to start up the struggle. The south had to be brought to the same level as the north and all that.

One day these Ideal Standard workers went out on strike, and we stopped too and talked to the union organisers. They were striking for an increase in the production bonus and they said that we were productive, too. And I said, No, we're just doing a course. No, you're productive, because they sell the units you make. You're not just doing a course, you're productive. A toilet bowl costs ten or fifteen thousand lire, it's not as if you're doing fuck all. This was fine by us, this discovery, we thought we'd been freeloading, living off the company. So we sat down outside too, and refused to go in.

Then the manager of Ideal Standard Salerno came to Brescia. He saw us sitting around outside and asked us what the hell we were doing. Yeah, we're on strike. But you're going in, aren't you? No, we've decided to join the struggle. Then after two days the workers from Brescia stop, but we decide to keep going. It was just us, twenty of us outside the gates, the others had gone in. While we were there a security guard came and called us: the manager wants to speak to you. We go in. Shit, the manager wants to speak to us, who knows, maybe they want to give us a pay rise.

We go in and he goes: Listen boys, down south there are lots of unemployed workers, you're not the only ones. We can throw you out right now. In fact, I already should have. Why did you go on strike? Did the union tell you to? Are you in the union? No, I said, do you have to be in a union to go on strike? Yes, you can only strike if you're in a union. If you strike and you're not in the union we can kick you out. Well, we didn't know that. We joined the struggle just like that, the other workers went on strike so we did, too.

Anyway, you want a pay rise, but did you know you're not producing anything? Did you know that in the factory in Salerno they started work a month ago and are already producing sixteen units, some even eighteen? And you lot here make fourteen and get paid more? We said that can't be true, that's impossible, that's a lie to make us stop. No, he says, I can end the course right now and send you back to Salerno. If you want to work, come and work, if not, get lost. We don't care. And we won't be giving you any pay rise.

Either I kick you out right now, or you all decide here and now to go back to work. If you do that I'll think about whether to send you back to Salerno or take you back on. So we discussed it among ourselves. I say, OK, it's better for us to be tough, isn't it? We say we don't want to work and so they kick us out. We'll go back down south, all twenty of us, and make trouble outside Standard. But some of them say they're married, that they want to finish the course as soon as possible. They want to work and earn money in Salerno, they don't want to make trouble. And so we decided to go back to work without having won anything.

After a month we finish the course and go home to Salerno. Well, there we discover that they were paying workers from Brescia, that is, workers from Ideal Standard at Brescia, with money from the Cassa del Mezzogiorno, with the excuse that they have to train the workers from Salerno. And that the workers were already producing more than us who'd done the course in Brescia. The factory had been in Brescia for thirty years and they made sixteen units a day. It had been at Salerno for two months and they were already making eighteen. They explained this by saying the factory was modern and the equipment was more efficient.

It was only because instead of lifting the units by hand, you lifted all the units together with a hoist. Some of the processes were automated, which at least saved your back. But something that was good for a worker's health cost you two extra units, that is, two more toilet bowls. I didn't go for that, thinking of the workers in Brescia who all had bad backs. They had their sides all strapped because they were getting muscle strains. And here, this new thing, using a hoist instead of your back to lift things, they'd done it to stop people going on benefits with pulled muscles. Which they made us pay for, by getting us to make two extra units. I mean, the new equipment in the new factories was only there so there were fewer workers but everyone produced more.

They didn't want to listen to reason. They said: Look, the others work, they make eighteen units. Everyone was making eighteen units, it was just me who only made sixteen. So they call me into the office. They say: listen, you seem like a good kid, but you have to change jobs. We should really sack you because you're not productive enough. But we'll send you to another section. They put me in another section, but for two days I had to stay in the old one, in the casting workshop. There were some units that had dried that I had to finish. I had to take them out of the moulds and finish the units that I was still working on.

I went back down from the office and found someone from the union who had been to ask for an increase in the piece rate. The management had given him the finger and this guy had said they'd have to go out on strike. As soon as I hear this I say: Great. And I join in with the union organiser shouting: Strike, strike. I go to my comrades in the casting workshop and I get them to leave. A supervisor comes and says: What are you doing here, this isn't your section? I say: Yes, it's still my section because I have to finish some units. So why don't you finish them? Because there's a strike, right? And the guy says nothing.

There were about fifty of us not working. They start to check who is still working. So we go to the guys who are still working and herd them out. The supervisors get pissed off and one of them threatens me. I was eating and I shoved my sandwich in his face. I'm jumping on him, my comrades are holding me back, they say: You've done the right thing, but that's enough. Then we go into the other sections and make them stop. We all go out into the yard and hold a meeting. We strike for fifteen days, with pickets day and night. Police vans all around. Then we march on the Salerno prefecture as well.

When we went back to work I was in a new section. I had to load finished units onto a line. Another guy checked them and two more put them onto trolleys. But to make up for the strike they decided to run two lines. Two checkers and two more packing. Whoever had to load the units onto one line now had to load them onto two. That is, it was me who had to do this double process. To make this work, they'd told the checkers, who checked whether the finished units were good or not, to speed up the checking. That is, if the guy in front didn't pack a unit, they were authorised to put it on the ground. Generally you can't put units on the ground, because they're easy to break.

They told me to keep putting new units on the line. To push the units up close together. But you can't put them close together, they might break, because they're made of porcelain, they're not meant to touch each other. And they authorised me to squash them up. I said: You're crazy, they'll break. And they replied: What do you care, do it the way you've been told. Their only concern was to increase production. The guy calls me a comrade, a unionist and he says to me: Listen, these people here want to make us work more. They want to put on two lines instead of one and then you'll have to bust your arse, you'll have to load both of them.

I tell my workmates who are packing and they say: Fuck, so we'll have to go slow. And they say to the checker: Why the fuck are you rushing? Take it slow. He says to them: No, I don't mind working like this. I spit in his face and go off to the bathroom for a piss. The supervisor of the kilns comes, a draughtsman. He says: You're breaking people's balls, be careful or we'll fire you. Yeah, I say, if your balls are so delicate you can keep them at home. Anyway, I go back to my workplace, and the checker kept going like crazy.

The next day I get to work and the security guards call me and hand me a letter. I open it and it says I've been sacked for fighting in the factory, for sabotage and I don't know what the fuck else. Because of that they weren't even paying me the eight days' notice and who knows what other entitlements. I say: Can't I go in? No, you can't go in any more. Now, I knew these security guards, one was the father of a friend, and I'd made friends with the other one. It didn't want to fight them,

I didn't have the stomach for it. At that moment I decided that if I ever went to work in a factory, wherever it was, I wouldn't ever make friends with the security guards.

I waited outside for the manager to come in so I could make him give me my money. But while I was there I needed a shit, so I went to have a shit and the engineer went past. To cut a long story short, I didn't get there in time to grab him. So then I went to the camera del lavoro[6] and I told them that they'd sacked me for these reasons. Ah, don't worry, we'll take care of it. We'll bring a nice little case. They'll have to give you everything. Anyway, they asked me if I'd joined the union. I said I'd signed up during the strike, I'd coughed up a thousand lire. OK, so they get me to do a letter to Ideal Standard. They get me to send it express and registered, I spend another two or three hundred lire. I wait about a fortnight: more than two weeks I waited for something to happen. I went to them and I said: Listen, I haven't heard anything more, and I need the money.

Well, you've got to be patient, don't worry. If they don't pay we'll bring a case against them and they'll give you everything. I got really jacked off with waiting. One morning I went and waited for the engineer to arrive at the factory. When he got there I jumped in front of his car. He stopped, I opened the door and slipped in as he tried to lock it. I put a hand on his shoulder and threw the letter in his face. I said:

Why didn't I get the eight days' in lieu of notice? You fired me and now I want to be paid. Not just the eight days, but the month of work I've missed, too.

I want everything, everything that's owed to me. Nothing more and nothing less, because you don't mess with me. He said: Listen, I wasn't there when you were fired. If it were up to me I wouldn't have fired you. You're a good lad, I would have moved you. If you want to come back to work I'll give you a better job, a job where you won't be like the others, a job just for you. I said positions at Ideal Standard didn't interest me any more. I've had it, I want my money right now, immediately. No more and no less than I'm owed. He says: Yes, don't worry. He takes me to the office, calls the clerks. He says: Work it out for him. Work what out? Everything, all of it. Really? Yes, everything, he says.

They work it out and I'm owed one hundred and twenty thousand lire. He calls me and says: Is one hundred and twenty thousand lire OK? I say: No. Then he says: Listen, with the accounts as they are, that's all I can give you. This is what we'll do: I'll get the supervisor to punch your timecard for the month of November. I'll get it punched for you so that next month you can come and collect your wages without working. OK, I say, that's OK by me. But no messing around. Next month I'll be back. I see you going by Fuorni every morning; I know where you live. So let's not mess around.

The engineer says: OK, but I want to tell you something. Get your head straight and I can find you another job.

He was from Brescia; he'd been transferred to Salerno. He didn't want to make too many enemies, apparently. He didn't want to lose sleep over thirty or forty thousand or a hundred thousand lire that wasn't his. What the fuck did he care about it? He even said he wanted to help me: I'll find you another job, he said. No, you don't understand. I don't want to work any more. I want to do nothing. And so I went and collected the money the month after and that was the end of the Ideal Standard story. I was unemployed for a while, but I bought nice shoes, an overcoat, some clothes. I spent all the money in less than a fortnight. I spent it all. I didn't have a single lira.

I didn't get unemployment benefit because I didn't have two years' worth of work stamps. But in the south the employment office was running building site schools—which was just a way to distribute money to people. They give you seven hundred lire a day. You go to the building site, which is not even a building site: it's an empty field where someone calls a roll. You say, Here, he marks the day down and you take off. Then on Saturday you go and collect the money, four thousand two hundred lire. And with that I could buy cigarettes, go to the movies, more or less manage to get by. As for whatever else I needed, I was living with my family.

One day I decide that was no good. I did the last of the summer work at Florio. There are lots of canneries there, mostly tomatoes. The work is seasonal. In the past this seasonal work lasted maybe three or four months. Now it's barely a month because there are fewer tomatoes. Anyway, I got a month at Florio, doing twelve hours a day, working Sundays. I made a hundred and fifty, a hundred and sixty thousand lire. I didn't even sign up for benefits because I decided I should go to Milano. Usually people who do the seasonal summer work get two or three or four months, even six months of benefits. They get fifteen hundred or two thousand lire a day. That's what they do when there's no work. They go on the dole.

Second chapter **Work**

I'm from Fuorni, which is a village near Salerno. There's Giovi, Caserosse, Mariconda, Pastena, Mercatello and so on. At the end of primary school my father and my mother were thinking of getting me to continue so they got some advice from the teachers. These teachers buttered up my father and mother. All parents should do this, they told them. They gave them some advice. It's better if he doesn't go to middle school. Apart from anything else, you have to pass the entrance exam. And you study more, the load is heavier. You need more books, it costs more. And then maybe he won't be able to finish, because it costs so much.

Your son can go to a trade school and then he'll be able to get a job in a factory. Be a foreman, a section head. The words foreman, section head sounded like a fairy tale, you didn't even really know what the fuck it was. How could we know, when there weren't any factories there yet? My father'd done a thousand different jobs. As the son of a peasant he had done everything, from smuggler after the war to labourer on building sites as he was now. And so it was decided that I should keep going to school. I was scared of going to high school, as it was called. Luckily I had friends from Fuorni who were going too.

We had to buy a bus pass, from Fuorni to the city. Right from the beginning there were divisions in the class, between the kids from the city and the kids from out of town. We came from Pontecagnano, from Battipaglia, from Baronissi, from Giffoni, from Nocera. The kids from the provinces were the so-called *cafoni*, hicks, the others were town kids. Some kids got used to this condition of inferiority. They tried to win over the kids from Salerno with ice cream, sweets, by lending a pen or a notebook.

Me and a friend from Pontecagnano preferred to meet this problem head-on. We went right at it with the kids from Salerno. We earned those kids' respect with our fists. Often when school got out there were punch ups, terrible battles. This went on for the whole first year of trade school. The second and third year were different. The difference wasn't between cafoni and town kids but between the smart kids and the dorks. We made fun of the dorks, we swiped their lunch and their money.

Next it was the discovery of the city, comparing life in the village with life in the city. I saw all these windows full of stuff. Trousers, bags, shoes, furniture, radios. I saw more stuff to eat in the grocers. On the newsstands I saw magazines with women on the covers: when I went back to the village I saw women with skirts down to their ankles. In the city I saw posters with women who were so different. I saw them in the street, going to the movies. They were all new things that stimulated my imagination. I felt like I was beginning to understand something. And then I discovered a basic thing: to dress well, to eat well, to live well, you needed money.

All this new stuff I saw in the city had a price on it, from the newspapers to the meat to the shoes; everything had a price. It wasn't like fruit on the trees in the village that we used to go and get of an evening, or the fish that we caught in the river. They weren't the clothes that our mothers gave us, which they made themselves or that came from who knew where — pants or shoes that we put on without even knowing what colour they were because we didn't give a fuck. There was a huge difference between the upbringing we'd had up to now in the village with our families, our peasant environment, and this city environment.

I discovered the importance of money then and began to ask for more money at home on Sundays. But bloody hell, they couldn't give it to me. They gave me a hundred or a hundred and fifty lire a week. And that was a lot, there really wasn't any money at home. Then I noticed something else. I saw all my friends, the ones who hadn't stayed at school. They weren't going into the fields with their parents to plant tomatoes, the way things had been since I was born. I had broken with the way we did things by going to school, but I saw that these guys had broken with it another way. Instead of going into the fields they went to work on building sites, and they made more money in two months than their parents made with a year's harvest.

They made more money than their parents and they wore jeans. At that time jeans were the most fashionable thing. They were the years when you saw movies like *Poveri ma belli.*[7] But if you went to school you didn't have a thousand or two thousand lire to buy jeans. The guys who had jeans also had pullovers, but not those pullovers that the shepherds wore up in the Apennines, in Irpinia, the hand-knitted ones. A pullover from a shop, lovely, in any colour. Then you bought a record player and records. Rock 'n' roll, rhythm and blues, all of that. And you danced like an American.

But you always needed money. Guys were already thinking of buying Lambrettas. This was exceptional, it broke with all the traditions of village life. Landowners had a horse and trap for going out on Sundays or going to town, or a bicycle, the type with high handlebars, and always black. And here were the sons of tomato farmers buying Lambrettas and all this other stuff.

That was when I started to say to my mother: Listen, I don't want to go to school any more, because I want jeans; I want to go to the movies, I want to go out for pizza. I want to go out and to do that you need money. If not, what am I going to do. I study, but then I'm stuck here wanting everything. It's no good living and wanting everything. I wanted to live immediately, right then. We were at the age when you start to have girlfriends and every Sunday we went dancing. My mother said: Listen, I'll tell you something. You're better, you're superior, because you go to school, you study. But I didn't listen, I didn't feel superior, I never had.

I judged superiority on the basis of things, on the basis of jeans, pullovers, record players, period. I didn't judge it on the basis of the bullshit they taught me at school, because look, that bullshit was no use at all for dancing, for going out, for eating pizza. So when my mother told me that I was superior, I didn't get it. I felt like it wasn't true at all.

One time we talk about it and my father is there, too. My father hesitates a bit. He thought that by sending me to school I would have a better life than his. Now that he saw that I wasn't a kid any more, that I was becoming a young man and had certain desires, he understood. But watch out, work's a bad thing, he told me. You have to get up early, you have to listen to the boss all the time. If there's no work you don't eat, if there is work you have to work hard. Work is never good. Work seems good to you because it will let you to go out for pizza, go dancing, go to the movies. But when you have a family you won't be going out for pizza, you won't be going dancing. You'll have to feed your family and then you'll see how tough work is.

This is why you have to think hard about it. I'm not telling you to go to school or to get a job. I'm only telling you one thing: work is bad, so try to avoid it. I send you to school because I think that's one way to avoid work. I felt this explanation, that work was a horrible thing, made more sense than what my mother had told me, that I was better. And I began to think that what my friends who'd gone to work in the building sites understood wasn't true, either: that money equals work, and that therefore work equals happiness. I began to have doubts about my discovery that happiness meant going to work on a building site.

It was as if, with this perspective on work and on his life, my father had said: See this family, see me, see yourself? Is this a happy family, your mother and I and your sisters? Poor, deprived, wretched, that's what we are. And then I understood that work is a fraud and nothing more, because in my family I didn't see any jeans, I didn't see any pullovers, I didn't see any record players. My father said: Here's a family, and here there's also work. Don't you think I work? And you can see what the result is.

I started to waver, I couldn't decide. Go to school or get a job? I'll get the record player and the pullover by working, but I'll end up like my father. Or go to school, which you could say might make me happier, in the sense that I wouldn't lead the life that I was leading with my family, the same life as my father and my mother and my sisters. And that was what made me keep going to school. I went to technical college because there were lower fees and fewer books, and the load was lighter: pretty much non-existent.

I did a three-year course in auto-electrics, a stupid thing because that's a trade you learn in the workshop. Young kids learned it by unscrewing globes and distributors. You need to know all the types of cars. But we learnt it all, you know, from books. We never saw the different types of batteries or distributors, ever. We learnt abstract things that were only useful for passing tests. But if a car blew a globe, a twelve-year-old kid from an auto-electrician knew how to fix it right away, and you didn't.

The only point of these technical schools was to give jobs to caretakers, headmasters and unemployed teachers. They were no use to us, spending money on textbooks and notebooks and lunches to go to school: they were expenses we couldn't afford. All that mattered was to know how to talk about the battery, the distributor, the dynamo, the starter motor. If you could talk about them, if you could remember what was in the book, you passed your tests. By then everyone was convinced that the fucking school was of no use at all, but if you talked to a teacher about it, naturally he denied it.

No, he'd say, that's ignorant. They're kids who only know how to do straightforward things. They do it but they don't understand why they do it. But you know what an electric current is, how it's created, how it flows. This is a superior fact. You'll go on to be foremen in the factories. They threw that in your face again, that you'd become a foreman. All of us, foremen, fifty or sixty of us, and all the technical schools in Italy turning out thousands of foremen every year. How many foremen did Italian industry need?

Finally I finished at this school where you didn't learn anything useful. And the teachers knew it too; no one failed the exams. When tech finished we all looked for jobs. We presented ourselves to the FIAT dealers, who had workshops. We spoke to them: What do you do? I'm an auto-electrician. But have you ever worked at it? No, but I studied it at tech. They never took us on. We went to Officine Mecchaniche, to Autobianchi, to Alfa, to Lancia. They didn't take us on; they didn't need us. They needed their youngsters who learnt everything there and who knew how to do everything. So we all went our separate ways, we never saw each other again. I don't think any of us ever worked as an auto-electrician or a foreman.

That summer I went to work in the tomato canneries. I worked twelve hours a day; I worked on Sundays too. I worked for two months and made nearly two hundred and fifty thousand lire. And with that money I bought an overcoat and other gear to get through the winter, though that wasn't enough. But I didn't go to work on the building sites like I had thought three years before. I saw the guys who had gone to work there and who were now turning eighteen and nineteen. Once you had the scooter, you stopped. Then you crashed the scooter, and you needed money to fix it. And for fines, and for petrol. And then the problem of getting engaged and married came up. You needed loads of money.

A whole lot of problems came up, and those guys didn't think too much about dancing and jeans then: they began to seem like second order problems. Sometimes they got fired. Work got tough. They started the piecework system. And then there was the fact that everyone was earning money. It was no longer the exception, a privilege like four or five years before. It was a need that became the same for everybody.

There was also a fixation: What's all this? You've been to school and now you want to be a worker? And so I couldn't do it. It was really a point of honour to not do certain work if you'd been a student. Then my parents had to support me so that I wouldn't have to go and work on a building site. When I worked in the tomato cannery they tried to keep it quiet, and so did I.

It was in those years that industrialisation started. The era of the development of the south started, partly to stop the labourers and the field hands rebelling because they weren't earning enough money to get by. So some industry started up. You could pay lower wages; there were no unions. People started working in the factories. But not too many, because they wanted most of them to leave for the north, to emigrate. But a little bit of money started to go around.

You saw cars, you saw fridges, television sets in people's houses. And I went to work in a factory for the first time, too. I went to Ideal Standard. And I discovered that what my father had told me was true: that work was just toil. It's a drag and that's all. So I was fired from Ideal Standard. And I thought about the avenue that was open to all southerners: that is, to emigrate, to go to Milano. To get myself up north, too, up where all these people were headed en masse: packed trains carrying away whole villages from the hinterland and the Apennines.

That wasn't the first time I'd been up north. I'd been there once before, straight after I finished tech, before Ideal Standard at Brescia. I went to Torino; I only stayed for a month. My married sister was there, the one who came back down every year for the holidays in a car. I was knocked sideways by that vast plain, by the work, by the mentality. And I came back in a hurry to go to the beach, to hang around with my friends. I went to my married sister's place in Torino and saw that they lived in a flat worse than ours in Salerno, a flat off the entranceway on the ground floor. One room where they slept and they ate. But they came down in a car, the jerks.

I went up by train. The train was so crowded I wanted to get off after only thirty kilometres. I did the whole journey standing up. Drunk people with pieces of bread this big eating in the passageways. Babies crying, shitting. Suitcases, packages, boxes everywhere. An incredible thing, and these people had already been travelling for ten hours. I got on at Salerno and they were coming from Sicily. They'd already been travelling since morning: they were totally pissed off. It was April. Down south the custom is to leave in spring, because everyone knows that before that it's cold up north. So people all leave in spring.

In Torino I worked as a metal polisher. A Fiat is nothing more than so many parts, so many accessories that someone makes. Actually no one makes them. For example, the handles on the 500 and the 600 are all made of aluminium; there's all this stuff made out of aluminium. Various foundries make them, then the foundries subcontract out the finishing. There's the clean-up at the foundry. You need to do a rough clean-up of the part, then you polish it with another buffer. There's a buffer for cleaning it up and a buffer that polishes it, with steel fibres. You polish the handle and it gets shiny and smooth. That was the job. They gave me the qualification of metal polisher.

There you had to finish two thousand units a day. I didn't have time to blow my nose. I was always black with dirt. I was a metal polisher. But I didn't like being a metal polisher and after a month I took off. I made back the money I'd spent that spring. But this time, the second time I went up north, I did it differently. I saw it wasn't true any more that you needed less money to get by in the south, that things cost less, the things that by now everybody was used to; a TV set or packaged meat cost the same in Salerno as in Torino. Petrol cost the same, a scooter cost the same, the train cost the same.

In the south the things that you needed were no longer cheaper. Yeah, up until five or six years ago you managed to get garlic, onions, chickens, fruit easily enough. You went into a field and took fruit, basil, onions. But now the fields were all fenced in and there were guards behind the fences. There were produce sellers who sold the produce, and if you went and stole it you ended up inside. And people were ashamed to show they were poor, so now you had to buy the fruit and vegetables that, one way or another, you used to get for free. It might have cost a bit less than in Milano or Torino. But there wasn't any money, there was much less money. So I decided to go up north because you really earned more money there.

I knew families up north. Whole families had left: one that lived right next door to me had all gone. The father had been a tomato farmer, he planted tomatoes at Versecca, an area on

32

the Sele plain. The sons were called Angelo, Rocco, Andrea, Armando, Carmine, Giovanni. They all worked together with their father on the tomatoes. All of them cutting reeds, all of them making ties; they used broom shoots to tie the tomato plants to the reeds so they'd grow up.

Then there was the custom of taking the tomatoes, cutting them in half and leaving them to dry in the sun. Then you pressed them through a copper sieve and out came the sauce, the concentrate, which you put into clay jars with fig leaves on top. That's how you made tomato paste, you made bottled tomatoes, too. Everyone made bottles. At lunch you ate tomato salad. In the evening, tomato salad; in the morning, tomato salad. Wine and that hard-baked bread they make there.

My father, on the other hand, was a casual worker. He made stakes out on the plain: he cut reeds in the meadows and sold them. You needed two or three hundred bundles of reeds a week. He sold them to the pasta factories for thirty thousand lire: the pasta factories put pasta to dry on the reeds; it was an ancient occupation that has disappeared now. My father did a bit of that, a bit of labouring on building sites. He turned his hand to all types of work. Quite often he was a carter, because he had a horse and cart. He got by however he could, but there was no way he would work as a farm hand, he wouldn't pick tomatoes: that was a terrible job.

Sometimes I used to help that neighbouring family with their tomatoes. My mother would say: Don't go—do you want to get mixed up with tomato growers? By now that family had all migrated, but they didn't go all together at the same time. The first to go was the second oldest brother, Andrea, who was the black sheep of the family. He was the kind of guy who always dodged work; out in the fields he'd find a nice cool spot, the type who didn't like work. He was illiterate, he hadn't wanted to go to school either. He left to do his military service and then never came back down.

Every so often a letter came. And then he turned up in the village, all smooth and with plenty of money. He said he sold flowers, because people bought flowers up north. To us that seemed crazy, people buying flowers. He said he sold flowers, and that on the day of the dead he made seventy or eighty thousand lire. We thought it was unbelievable. Now he was trying to open a flower shop. He was getting a drivers licence, he wanted to buy a van to get flowers from San Remo and bring them to Milano: things that were like fairy tales to his brothers and his friends.

He told us these stories too; in the evenings we used to sit outside our houses, under a grapevine. Now they've paved it all over, there's no grass there now. Sitting there of an evening we used to talk. So Andrea told us these stories about what he'd got up to up north. About three or four years after

Andrea had gone away and been back a couple of times to visit his family, another brother, Rocco, left. This guy Rocco was one of the youngsters that everybody in the village talked about. He was the type who gave the finger to the landowners. He was the type that landowners don't like, the type who bought new clothes, too. At that time, if someone bought new clothes, the bosses and the landowners looked on it badly. They gave you a hard time because you had new clothes.

This guy Rocco was sick of life in the fields with his father, and he took off as well, to Milano. When he gets there they are building the Metro and he gets a job driving an excavator. Every now and again he wrote. When a letter came from someone who was away, the first thing you did was read it to the family. Then you let all the neighbouring families who knew the guy read it. It became a thing in the village: what he had written, what he said, what was new. You knew the postman had been with a letter: Who's it from, your son? What's he say? What's new?

There wasn't TV or movies like today or a newspaper with all the news in it. Before, letters were the most important way of getting news around. You would talk about a letter for a week or more. Then another one would arrive and on you'd go. That's how I heard that Rocco was driving an excavator in Milano. And I couldn't imagine what the fuck this excavator was. It must have been a really fine thing to drive an excavator.

In a rural village the only thing you knew about were hoes and oxen.

Rocco wrote that he was working twelve hours a day, which didn't impress anyone because in the fields you worked maybe fourteen; there was no work schedule. And he was making, I don't know, some fantastic sum. Naturally his father was happy. Rocco was engaged to a girl from a nearby village and after a year and a half he comes back to get married. He shows up in the village wearing a black suit, with a white shirt, a black tie, black shoes. He turns up looking really smart, and everyone was looking at him. He had a suitcase too, not the usual box tied up with a bit of string that you took up north. And the landlord of the building where he lived, and where we lived too, called him over. He says: How are you, how are things going. He gave him a dirty look, from head to toe.

Then all the landlords and landowners were talking about him in the evening when they went to the barbers for their shave. In the village, labourers and farmhands who were at the barber's had to make way if a landlord or landowner arrived for a shave. The barber took out a new, clean towel, whereas for everyone else he used the same towel all day. They changed them the next day, because they were filthy. But for the landlords they got a clean towel. And the beauty of it is that the landlords didn't even pay for a shave, while everyone else had to pay.

The landlords talked in the barber shop: Have you seen Rocco, he's back. Yeah, he's doing well, why don't you all go away too? And the labourers said: Come on, up there you don't live so well. There's fog, the air is bad. We're not going, only fools go. That guy thinks he's something, with his clean clothes. That is to say, the landlords didn't make these landlord-type judgements, the others did, the ones who stayed behind. The landlords only stoked the fires. They were checking to see how it went down, a country boy coming home got up like that, when they didn't even have clothes like that. It bothered them, this fact; it spoiled things. The only thing the landowners said was: But he's a good type, he's got it right. There's no doubt about that, the labourers said.

When he got married Rocco brought a suit for his father and clothes for his mother and brothers. All of them with new clothes, everyone looking at this family with new clothes. It was stuff that you couldn't get in the village, only in the city. There were waiters at the wedding who brought around sweets, champagne, the lot. And music. But a wedding in the south, for peasants, has always been a big deal, a mark of having arrived. People went into debt to get married, and spent the rest of their lives paying it off.

As things got worse for this family, they went away one after the other. All the brothers went, and Rocco found them jobs. Up north they did well, they got married and all the rest of it.

In the end they all left, including the parents. There were lots of families that did the same; this is the family I remember best because I knew them. They were our neighbours, they lived right next door to us. And I decided to go up north too, because there was money up there.

Third chapter **The north**

Anyway, I took off up north. In Milano the first thing was to go and find this guy Rocco, because he was a reference point for me, something secure. Rocco was 20 years older than me. I remember that he was already a man when I was a little kid. He was the kind of guy people were always talking about. He was a stirrer, they said, someone who wanted to see himself as equal to the bosses and the landlords. He'd come from nowhere and gone up north, and he'd made it there. He was a role model for any youngster who wanted to leave the village. He lived in Corsico, a town near Milano. When he saw me he asked how my mother was and how my sisters were. He opened the fridge and got a couple of beers. He asked me a heap of questions; he was offering me drinks, really happy to see me.

Then he says to his wife: make some steaks. He asks me: how much will you eat, a little or a lot. He was a healthy type, he liked to eat and drink. He liked to have whatever he wanted, and now he had it. He started to talk about when he was down south. He says: We had it tough down there, because the landowners are all ignorant. Who knows who the fuck they think they are just because they have a little bit of land. They don't understand that it's us workers who make everything. If it wasn't for us they'd starve. Now they're finished, they're bums, because they didn't want to do the right thing by the people.

He went on like that. Here, on the other hand, he said, when I arrived the bosses put themselves at my service. They let me stay in the hut, eating and sleeping for free. I worked on the excavator and they paid me as a jobber: you know, the more I worked, the more they gave me. Down south, however much you worked they still only gave you what they wanted to, you never knew what you were getting. They had it all worked out, the bastards. Southerners are stupid, they don't understand anything. Here everyone's equal, boss and workers. Sure, there's the difference that he has more money and that he's in charge in his factory.

But I eat, too, I have a house, too. You see this house — it's mine; I've got a car, a truck, the excavator. What I mean is, I'm a boss too. Everyone is a boss at his own level here. Of course there's the worker who doesn't have anything, who works in a factory. But he has rights, he gets holidays, insurance and all of that. The thing is, it's not as if you're badly off here. As long as you have a job, you're all right. You don't have to worry about anything. Rocco made this big argument in favour of Milano and the north.

I stayed there a while talking to Rocco, then I asked about his younger brother Giovanni, the one who was three years older then me; we were almost the same age. He works in a factory nearby, he said. He hasn't knocked off yet, but he'll be here around nine. He's a bit of a slacker, Rocco said. He must have the same mentality as you. You've all got the same mentality, you guys. He's already quit three jobs. He doesn't get it: here you have to stick at one job. You need to figure out where you can work to get ahead. Changing jobs all the time isn't the way to get ahead. I've always been with the same firm and I work for myself. For myself, but always with the same firm.

Anyway, I said, I really have to get a job. I need a job right away. I'm not thinking of making a career or anything at the moment. So what do you want to do, he said, what would you like to do? You need to get a job in a factory, you need to try and make a bit of money. Without changing jobs all the time, otherwise you'll never make anything. Then Giovanni turned up, we said hello, talked about Fuorni, Salerno, Pontecagnano. About friends we knew, about girls and all that. And then he says: sleep here. Come to work with me tomorrow, and tomorrow night we'll find a pensione for you.

The next day Giovanni took me to work. The factory was near Zingone[8] and they made this stuff called celegno. They made all these cut-out pieces that were stuck to furniture as ornaments. They look carved, but they're actually a composite of sawdust and PVA. It looks like real wood, but they call it celegno. I started working at this craft kind of thing, and I was staying in a pensione with a couple of other migrants. They were all immigrants in this town, there wasn't anyone

41

from there. Even the northerners were immigrants, some from Brescia, some from Bergamo and so on.

There was a Lucanian[9] in this pensione who worked twelve hours a day on a building site. He cooked for himself at night, spent fifty lire a day tops but earned about seven or eight thousand. He was always economising, he never went out at night or on holidays. After three or four months this guy had six or seven hundred thousand lire in the bank. He showed me his bank book and said he wanted to buy a car. When spring came I started to be late every morning. I was pissed off with it, I wanted to get back down south and go to the beach. I figured out that I'd worked the whole winter, and I'd be owed thirty or forty or maybe even fifty thousand lire in severance pay, plus eight days notice, a week's pay that I'd worked, all up around a hundred thousand lire if they fired me. With that I'd be able to go back down south and stay a while without doing anything.

I started coming late every morning. At a certain point they get pissed off and threaten to fire me if I'm late the next day. I'm late again and they fire me. They give me the severance pay, the eight days in lieu of notice, the week I've worked and I go back down to go to the beach. Then summer came but the money ran out after the first month. It was the end of April when I went down, in May the money was already gone. June, July, August and September I stayed down there. At first I worked a little in a place where they carved wood for coffins. Then I spent the summer months working as a lifeguard. There are these beach setups where you help with painting and setting up the cabins. When it's set up you put the umbrellas up every morning, rake the beach, that kind of thing.

That's how I spent the whole summer. At the end of summer I went back up to Milano. But this time I didn't want to stay out in the suburbs. Staying in the suburbs I spent even more money, because every night I'd go into Milano. Between transport and other things I'd spend a lot more, and I wouldn't enjoy myself at all out in the suburbs. So I decided to stay right in Milano. As soon as I got to Milano I left my suitcases at the station and looked for a pensione downtown. I found one in via Pontaccio, right near Brera, via Solferino, via Fatebenefratelli, that neighbourhood.

That was the centre of town. You could stay in the bars until three or four in the morning; all up, it was a lot of fun. And you could eat in the bars. There's one called Gran Bar and you can eat there too. Instead of eating in a restaurant and spending money, and spending more money to go to a bar, I ate a plate of pasta or a fior di latte or something at Gran Bar. I spent seven or eight hundred lire and stayed all night. There was some fantastic pussy hanging around that part of town. Fags, pimps, junkies, black marketeers, hippies; a great environment.

Then I decided to get some qualifications. I said, fuck it, I have to study, there's work here, there's schools. And I wanted to study, I was obsessed with studying, I wanted to go to art school. At the Castello Sforzesco there were evening art classes. I went to enrol; you paid a hundred and fifty lire to apply. I went to do the exams, which took three days. There were prisms, cubes, spheres, that kind of thing. You had to draw them, then they assessed you on the drawings.

But actually they assessed you on other things. They asked what you did for work, if you lived in Milano with your family and so on. And in effect they took people who didn't know how to draw at all, but who were young and lived with their families or who worked. But seeing I didn't have a job, they didn't take me, because they thought I wouldn't finish the course, or that there was no point in me doing it, or something like that. It wasn't lack of ability, that I didn't know how to draw, because I'd shown them that I knew how to draw. So given that I didn't manage to get into school to get a diploma, I decided that the only worthwhile thing was living the life.

I said, what fucking use is a diploma? No way am I interested in learning a trade. It's obviously useful for making more money, to have a more comfortable life. But the most comfortable life means working as little as possible, eating well, getting laid. All right, I thought, I can do these things without a diploma, the main thing is to work as little as possible and

44

to make money as quickly as possible. So I decided to do exactly that. I found a job on a building site. After a while I got pissed off with it and I got drunk and didn't go to work in the afternoon, so they fired me and I went for a while without doing anything.

I had a bit of ready money and I just hung around. Not like the year before at Corsico. Free time at Corsico was crazy: a town with two dance halls, three or four cinemas, the parish cinema. People meeting up in bars, playing cards or talking about sport. And the young girls, daughters of southerners who had the usual southern habit of taking a walk together while the boys waited for them somewhere out of the way to maybe lay them up against a tree. But there was no real rapport between people. If you had money to spend in the bar you were in, you were someone. The more you spent, the better you dressed, the more friends you had. If not you were left out, and that pissed me off.

The city, on the other hand, for me, someone born in the provinces in a tiny village, was the ultimate place for all kinds of experiences. In the pensione where I was staying I saw people coming all the time, waiters, students, painters, jerks, bricklayers. There were all kinds of people of all races coming and going in that pensione. Then, going down to the bar I'd meet the type of people you saw in the newspapers, actors, singers: there were loads of singers hanging around there. There were those guys from the comic strips, the semi-pornographic ones like Men and Bolero. And there were lots of women and lots of actor types who hung around via Brera.

I felt a provincial kind of pleasure, seeing all those people right there. Ah, they're here, they're alive, they're jerks like me. I wanted to be friendly with them, I was hoping to see what the fuck they were like. I was always there waiting, but in fact if I wanted to get laid I went with the hookers who were always hanging around. I never managed to make it with any of the women I met in bars, even though I was always ready for any kind of adventure. I was always ready, I hung around those places, Gran Bar, another one, what was it called, Jamaica. And then there were all kinds of students to talk to and discuss things with as well.

A lot of others, on the other hand, especially the painters, messed with you. They spoke French or English, even if they were Italian; if you knew French or English it showed that you had travelled or studied. In places like that they did this to show they were different, speaking French or English so they didn't have to mix, to avoid types like me as far as I could see. But one night I was drinking with a friend who knew German, someone I had worked with at Alemagna, and we managed to raise a bit of hell. Someone was playing a guitar, and we were drunk and we started to sing in German, or rather, he sang in German and I just made a lot of noise. We met this character who wanted us to be furniture salesmen or cigarette smugglers. This guy was into everything, except he was a real prick. But I didn't have a driver's license; I didn't know how to drive.

Another night I met a junkie who wanted the key to get in so she could go to bed, she was calling to a friend from outside the pensione. I went down, she was out of it, I started to kiss her. She said: What, you want to get laid, but I don't feel like it. This world seemed so strange to me; I liked this way of life that had nothing to do with factories, with the countryside, with religion. It was a world apart from the one I knew, which I liked. I was up for anything, even if I only ended up at the movies. Or if I ended up being a bit of a sleaze by trying to hook up with foreign women in the street or girls in dance halls, in the bars.

It was the same thing with wanting to go to night school. I thought I might be able to meet girls who went to art school and get a bit friendly with them. I was looking for ways to make some moves, because in a city if you stay on your own you never manage to do anything, you're stuck. You need a circle of friends, especially of women friends, to get on, to get rich. There were a lot of messed-up people in Milano, especially girls from small towns who ran away from home and came to Milano because they wanted to hang out with the hippies. One time I brought one of them up to the pensione but the landlord threatened to kick me out. Then I found a job at Alemagna.

So I meet a girl who works in a factory, but she said she was a secretary. I didn't care, I didn't even like her. If I'd been down south I wouldn't even have given a shit about her. It's just that in Milano these bitches were used to getting someone to pay for everything. They sold themselves just like prostitutes, these girls, these wage-earners. But I went with this one because she paid her way and I paid mine. I was with this girl and I took her up to the pensione where I was living. But the landlord kicked me out the next day because he had already warned me not to take anyone up to my room. You weren't allowed to take anyone up to your room. If you wanted to get laid you had to go to a hotel, you couldn't bring a girl into the pensione. The pensione was only for sleeping. And so I got kicked out of the pensione, too.

I'd made a friend at Alemagna and I went to stay at his place. I couldn't handle working any more, I was fed up with it, and I went from one friend to another to eat. I went to visit them in turns. These friends liked me because I didn't work much and I had a lot to say, and so I managed to go to the movies and to eat. In the evenings I went to wait for this girl to finish work, then we went for pizza. Anyway, that's how I got by. And then I hung around the bars looking for someone who wanted me to work the black market or some other way of making money quickly, or to find a woman to fuck. I kept myself ready for any kind of adventure.

All I found was an engineer who wanted me to guard a yacht he kept at Viareggio. Anyway, I'd acquired a heap of debts and quite a lot of friends in Milano. And in the house where I was living, my Sicilian friend's place, I'd become quite good friends with his wife. It bothered me that he might realise and I thought of slipping away from Milano. In Milano I'd tried all kinds of work; sometimes I worked in the porters gangs. I went to some office, worked for two or three days, I threw myself into all kinds of things. I applied to Fiat to get away from Milano, because I had so many debts. I was starting to give my friends the shits, apart from this friend I'd made when I worked at Alemagna.

Alemagna is a place where they give you a contract for a month or two, up to four months. I had a contract for two months and I started working in November. They gave us a hat like the ones cooks wear, an apron and a pair of pants. They gave us a more or less hygienic uniform. I was fired from there in a rather strange way. I was in a section where they made dough, and then they mixed it with this machinery. When the dough came out they put these plastic carts under it, like great big basins. The dough went in, we had to put a little flour in first, then the dough sat there to rise. It was pretty light work, all told.

One day I was reading Diabolik in the pensione and I forgot that I had to go to work. It hit me at the last minute, I ran down, got on the Metro, arrived late. When you were late, even a couple of minutes, they docked you half and hour, they paid you half an hour less, so I decided to go in half an hour late. I went to have a shot of grappa, I got changed calmly, figuring I'd stamp my timecard a minute before the half-hour was up. Two minutes or half an hour late, it was all the same.

Where you clocked on there was a kind of large glass cabin with warning lights for the ovens and all the sections. There were a couple of supervisors, and an Alemagna manager, the manager of my section. As I was going past he waves to me. I say: Yes, sir, what is it? Please adjust your hat, he says. It was a tall hat and I'd squashed it, I was wearing it like one of those Sardinian caps, a Sardinian shepherd's cap. I was wearing it down over my eyes, with my hands in my pocket, and I was half an hour late.

So he gets a little pissed off and he says: Adjust your hat. No, it's OK like this, why should I adjust it? Adjust it. And I kept on walking. He comes out of the cabin and says: Why are you late? Eh, I don't remember why I'm late, I don't know, I'm just late. You can be late for all kinds of reasons, I don't remember. What do you mean, you're late and you don't know why? It's because I forgot I had to come to work. Oh, you forgot that you had to come to work. This is quite serious. Well, do you know that now I'm going to suspend you for a day?

I say: Listen either you fire me, or I'm going to work. I don't deserve a day's suspension because I was half-an-hour late, and I won't take it. So either you fire me and tell me the reason why, or I'm going to work. I don't deserve a day's suspension and I'm not taking it. He says I have to leave, I call him a jerk and go off to work. He sends a security guard from upstairs to find out my name, then two more arrive and ask where I am. I say: Here I am. I warn these guys: Listen, if you want to send me away by force don't try, because I might end up in jail but I'm not going that way. If they want to get rid of me they have to give me a month's pay, because I have a contract for two months and I've only done a month, I'm due another month's pay.

But it's only a one-day suspension, they say. No, I'm not up for a day's suspension and I'm not taking it. Anyway, they say, go and talk to the boss in the office. I go, sit myself down in the office, the boss arrives, he says: What are you doing sitting there? Eh, I'm sitting here because I'm waiting for you. What do you want with me? You had better shift yourself and get out of here. I say: Wait a minute. They want to suspend me for a day, but I don't deserve it. I was half an hour late for the first time and I don't think a one-day suspension is right for being half an hour late.

No, he says, that's not why, it's because you called the director a jerk. But that's impossible, I didn't call him a jerk, he
obviously didn't hear me right. I can't help it if the director
is deaf and doesn't understand what someone says. All I said
was I was going to work, and that I wasn't leaving. Anyway,
you have to go, he says. And if you don't go, I'm calling the police. Fine, call the police. I'll go to jail but I won't give you the
satisfaction of a suspension I don't deserve because there's
no reason for it. If you fire me you have to give me a month's
pay, plus eight days' notice. Oh, we'll see about that. Yes, we
will see.

The guy makes a phone call and sends me to another office,
where they prepare the documents, my work book, a letter
where I give notice, all of that. They tell me to sign it. I say:
I'm not signing anything; first I want to see the money and
then I'll sign. They tell me: Listen, don't be smart or this will
work out badly for you. You'll end up inside for real and you
won't get a cent. I say: Look, that's my business. I understand
what life's about, what work's about, I really don't care if I
end up inside.

But I had it all worked out. They couldn't arrest me for that
kind of thing. Alemagna couldn't afford to look as crap as
they would if an episode like this ended up in the newspapers:
A worker arrested because he refuses a one-day suspension.
And because they wouldn't want that kind of hassle, I was

pretty sure I wouldn't end up inside and that I'd even get all the money. The jerk insisted; he threatened me a little and made out he was looking out for me: So where are you from? I'm from Salerno. Hey, I'm from down that way too, I'm from Avellino. He made out he was one of us, like he was looking out for me. He offered me cigarettes, then he went on: If you sign it, you'll be able to apply to Alemagna some other time and they'll take you on again. But if you go on like this they'll never take you on here again.

I say: Fuck, there's so much of that kind of work I really don't need to bother with Alemagna. You have to work, but you don't have to be taken for a fool, and here they really want to treat me like a fool. What, I have to do whatever the director says to get work here again? I'm really not interested in that. The director has made a mistake, and I'm not interested in a day's suspension. Now they want to fire me. Even better; pay me the month. The guy starts calling other offices, I don't know, admin, personnel and so on. The management was insisting on the telephone: hang tough, threaten him again, then you'll see. From three o'clock until seven o'clock, four hours of argument and drama.

The office workers' nerves were shredded. I didn't move, didn't leave the office, the guy was there with the paperwork ready, and they went on working out what they owed me. Every half hour they brought a slip of paper with a new figure written on it. Eighty thousand. And what's eighty thousand, I say. It's the rest of the month plus eight days' notice. And what's that got to do with it? You have to give me another month's pay, another eighty thousand apart from last month's money and the eight days' notice. So that'll be a load of money, not just eighty thousand lire.

A drama that went on and on; the office girl was getting hysterical: Get him out! We can't work any more! I say: I don't give a shit, you can go on strike if you don't want to work as far as I'm concerned. I don't care; I just want my money. He calls again, says: this guy's a real hard-ass, he's not giving in, the clerks are pissed off, they don't want to keep working. We just have to give him the money; if not, I'll call the police, because I just can't go on. What do you mean, call the police? Yes, I'll call the police. Well tell him that, they said from the other end of the line, which I could hear because I was right there behind him.

He comes over to me again: Listen, if you don't take the money I swear, I swear on my father, on my children, on my children's health, that I will call the police. I say, so call the police. That way we'll be finished with talking. Because I don't want to discuss it with you. You want to rip me off, what the fuck have we got to talk about, you and me? I've told you that I want the money, I don't want to discuss it, it's you who wants to discuss it with me. I'm not pissing you off, if anything you're pissing me off. He phones again and says: Listen, I give up. I'm telling the clerks to give him everything because I can't take any more. This guy's a real hard-ass and there's nothing else for it.

OK, do whatever you want, you hear over the phone from the other end, because he was calling right in front of me. Then he goes to me: OK, you've won, see? You're a real hard nut, well done, you've done it. Sign here. I say: Just a minute. First I want to see the money. Without the money I won't sign anything. He gets the clerk to give him the papers, the work book, and he takes me to the pay office. They give me the rest of the month, the eighty thousand of the month still to come and the eight days' notice. I sign everything and I exit Alemagna. Because of the director's stupid remark I managed to get myself a month's pay without working for it.

Alemagna was in effect my second factory job in Milano. After two months' work on a building site and a month at Alemagna, I was short of work. I worked in these day labourers' gangs. They sent you to Siemens, to SIP, to Standa, wherever there were goods to unload. Even factories that needed workers for certain tasks went to these day labourers' gangs, which was really a form of legal casualisation.

For a while I did that kind of work. The only thing was, sometimes I didn't get any. I went looking for that kind of work, for money when I didn't have anything in my pockets, and sometimes I ran the risk of not finding any. One time when I was really broke, I only had a thousand lire left, I went looking for work. It was Friday, and I didn't find anything. On Saturday they don't hire — we'll talk about it on Monday. So Friday, Saturday, Sunday and Monday, four days and I only had a thousand lire. I ended up eating on Friday, and on Saturday I didn't eat all day. On Sunday morning I thought about going to give blood.

One of my friends had told me that they'd given him three thousand five hundred lire for giving blood. So I thought about giving blood myself, so that I'd make three thousand five hundred lire and could eat. I had a cappuccino to raise my blood pressure. In Milano you always have to have something to keep yourself going. I had a cappuccino at San Babila, in the Motta bar, opposite the transfusion caravan that's always in Corso Vittorio Emanuele, between San Babila and the portico. I went in and took off my shirt.

They examined my chest and took a bit of blood from my finger. They took an X-ray and did the test to see if you have syphilis. Then they took my blood pressure, and it was really low. They asked me how old I was, if I'd had any diseases, what work I did. I'm unemployed, I said. These jerks asked me what diseases I had, without asking me if I'd eaten; a thing like that wouldn't have entered their minds. They saw that I was twenty-five, that I had low blood pressure, that I was unemployed and it didn't even cross their mind that I might be starving.

They laid me on the bed, slipped the needle in and only a little blood came out. In fact it didn't even half fill a flask, and then no more came out, it coagulated. They were scared when they saw no more blood was coming out; generally when you put the needle in blood spurts into the flask and fills it up in a minute, a minute and a half tops. I'd been there for three minutes and the flask wasn't even half full and no more blood was coming out. They were a bit worried, so I said to the doctor: Listen, I need some money, at least a thousand lire. Why? Because I haven't eaten and I'm hungry. Oh, you haven't eaten, we're sorry. We can give you some coffee and some Motta Buondí.[10]

In effect I knew that you donated blood to AVIS,[11] but I thought that if someone wanted money they paid, they gave you some money. Because all told you had given them goods, it's not as if you hadn't given them anything. The doctor told me: No, you donate blood here. It seemed strange to me, this obligatory donation. He said: Anyway, have some coffee. I didn't eat the Motta Buondí, because I had worked at Alemagna, and I knew how I used to handle the cakes there. All up I didn't have any great faith in Motta's Buondí.

Anyway I had got to the point of suffering from hunger in Milano, and I also had a load of debts to friends and people from back home. And then there was the thing with my Sicilian friend's wife where I was living. So I didn't want to stay in Milano any more and I decided I needed a change of scene. I applied to Fiat, and then a letter came calling me in so I went off to Torino. Everyone had told me that at Fiat you did well, there were holidays, all kinds of things. I didn't care so much about that, it was because I'd burnt all my friends in Milano, all my connections. I thought that by going to Fiat and earning a salary I could get myself straight, then I'd see.

And in Torino I could stay at my sister's place. Lots of other migrants who came straight from the south stayed with friends or relatives, or they had the address of some pensione or little hotel. But there were some unlucky ones who spent a few days in the station, and lots even a month, in the second-class waiting room at Porta Nuova. It was patrolled by police who made sure that journalists didn't get near it. To get into the second-class waiting room at Porta Nuova at night you had to show your Fiat ID card if you were already working there, or the letter from Fiat that said you should come for an interview. Without it the police wouldn't let anyone into this dormitory that Fiat had, for free, at Torino station.

Fourth chapter **Fiat**

Before Fiat, politically I was a qualunquista,[12] cynical about politics. Now I saw these students handing out leaflets at the gates of Fiat, wanting to talk to the workers. This seemed a bit strange. I asked myself, Why is this, they're free to sleep around and enjoy themselves. They come to the gates of a factory, which is the most disgusting thing there is: a factory, which really is the most absurd and disgusting thing there is. They come out the front here, what are they doing? This fact made me a little curious. Then in the end I thought they were crazy, dickheads, missionaries, and I didn't take any interest in what they said.

This was in the spring, in April. I'd never been to the meetings with the students. One time I went to May Day. I had never got May Day — la festa del lavoro: what a joke, the festival of work. The workers' festival, the workers who celebrate a festival. I didn't get what the festival of workers, or the festival of work, meant. I didn't get why work should be celebrated. It's like, when I didn't work I didn't know what the fuck to do, because I was a worker, that is, someone who spent the greater part of his day in the factory, and with what was left all I could do was rest up for the next day. But that holiday I went to May Day on a whim, to listen to a rally of I don't know who.

And I saw all these people with red scarves and flags. I heard them saying things I already knew. It's not like I was from Mars. I knew them even if I didn't understand them. And out in front of the smart bars in the piazza were the bourgeoisie. And there was the petite bourgeoisie, the peasants, the merchants, the priests, the savers, the students, the intellectuals, the speculators, the clerks and the various arselickers. Listening to the union officials' speeches. And there between the unionists in the middle of the piazza and the bourgeoisie out the front of the bars, there was this mass of workers, another race. And between the bourgeoisie and the workers there was this big display of Fiat cars.

A festival, that is, a fair. I listened to the union officials. Comrades, we can't just say these things today in the piazza. We have to say them and do them tomorrow in the factory. And I thought, yeah, this guy is right. It's useless celebrating, only acting up when they let us into the piazza with the red flags. We have to do it in the factory, too.

Then I went off and saw another demonstration where they were chanting Mao Tse Tung Ho Chi Minh. I asked myself, who are these guys. More red flags, more signs. But I didn't know anything about that then. I was in the dark. Some weeks later I stumbled on a meeting of these students at a bar near Mirafiori. Anyway it had been a few days since I started to stir things up in the factory. I was in workshop 54 of the body

60

plant, on the 500 line. I'd been there for a month, since the day after the interview I did to get into Fiat.

At the interview there were two thousand of us; everyone got a number and they asked us these bullshit questions. Proforma questions, the same for everyone. As there were so many of us, the poor clerks who asked the questions went through us fast. They looked you in the eye and fired off a couple of quick questions. You answered something and they said: Go to the next room. And everyone went to the next room. In the next room a guard with a list called us out twenty at a time and took us to another room where they did the medicals.

First there was an eye test. Look here, close your eye, look up, read there, all that kind of thing. Then hearing, whether you could hear properly. Lift your right leg, lift your left leg. They checked your teeth, nose, eyes, ears, throat. And between one examination and the next it was two o'clock. At two o'clock they told us we could go and eat. For this first day's physical we had to go on an empty stomach. Nothing to drink, nothing to eat, because we had to have a blood test. Some managed to have the blood test done before two o'clock, others didn't. The guys who had to go back in the afternoon for their blood test didn't eat at two. They'd been fasting from the night before.

At the blood tests there was a stench you could smell from outside the door. Inside were thousands of vials of blood. Blood-soaked cotton balls everywhere. On one side a heap a metre-and-a-half high of cotton, red with blood. They took blood, and it hurt because they weren't bothering where they stuck the needle. They stuck the needle in wherever and drew. Then they put the vial to one side and threw the bloodstained cotton ball onto the heap on the other.

From there we went to another room where a nurse handed us a jar. There were only two booths for pissing. We got into a circle and set about pissing in our jars. We said we were making beer and had a laugh. Then we put our jars up on top and the nurse asked us our names and wrote them on a sheet of paper under the number of each jar.

The next day was the general physical. You had to lift weights. There was this machinery with weights attached. They were checking how strong we were. This physical took two hours because there were two thousand of us and all two thousand of us had to take it. Not everyone got through it that day and they had to come back the next day, six or seven hours for this physical. After you had passed it you had to wait for the general medical. You stripped naked.

You were standing there naked in front of this quack. He's sitting in a white smock, asking you questions. What's your name, how old are you, if you'd done your military service, if you had a girlfriend. Then he made you march, forward, turn around, raise your arms, lower your arms, get down on the floor, show your hands, show your feet, the soles of your feet. Then he looked at your balls, whether you had any, all that kind of thing. Say thirty-three, cough, inhale, all of this bullshit. A whole day to do this physical, because it took a quarter of an hour each to do it and there were two thousand of us.

Then the quack says to me: Have you had any surgical procedures? You could see very well that I had never had any surgical procedures, because, thank God, I didn't have a mark on me. Yeah, yeah, I go, on my left ball. How did it happen? This guy was unhappy because he hadn't noticed it before. I said to myself, now I'm going to make this doctor look stupid. I was playing soccer, I replied, and I got a kick in the balls and they had to operate on me.

Really? OK, you'll have to come for a check-up tomorrow. Another guy said he'd had a broken arm and he had to come the next day too. The point of this, as I see it, was to get into the worker's head that he had to be healthy, whole and so on. I don't know what the fucking point of it was: they took us all anyway. Even guys who couldn't hear, who wore glasses, who were lame or who had an arm in plaster. Everyone, absolutely everyone down to the last man; maybe they wouldn't have taken a paraplegic.

We went in again the next day for the check-up. They sent me to a room where there was a quack who didn't even have a white smock on. He only had a lovely blonde secretary who waggled her arse back and forth around the room. She brought him my file and he sat himself down on a stool. He made me drop my pants and then he felt my balls. Where did you have the operation? On this one here. Get dressed. I pulled my pants up and he didn't say anything. The lovely secretary gave me some papers saying I should report to Fiat in two days.

Everyone who passed the physical was at Fiat two days later. That is, all of us. Someone from the hiring office came right away. Or from public relations, a psychologist or a social worker, who knows who the fuck it was. He arrives and says: Friends. I welcome you to Fiat on my own behalf and on behalf of the management who have taken you on. Good, well done. All of us clapping. The personnel department, he says, is open to Fiat employees who have children, who have personal problems, social problems to resolve, all that type of thing. If you need money, ask us for it. Ah, says some Neapolitan or other, I need ten thousand lire. No, not like that, you can ask for a loan when you're working, if you have real needs. For now you have to sort these things out yourselves. When you're working you can ask for a loan.

64

Then they turned us out of the offices into the actual Fiat factory. Another character, an office worker, took our numbers and gave us other numbers. Locker room number, corridor number, locker number, workshop number, line number. To do all this they had us for half the day. Then we went into the big boss's office, the chief engineer of the body plant. We went in a few at a time; apparently he asked everyone the same questions, made the same speech, the same words for everybody.

I welcome you all to Fiat. You know what Fiat is, Fiat is everything in Italy. If you have read anything bad in the communist press about the assembly line, that's all lies. Because here the only workers who aren't happy are the slackers, those who don't want to work. The rest all work and are happy to work and lead good lives. They all own cars, and Fiat has creches for our workers' children. And there are discounts in some shops if you're a Fiat employee. He gave us this whole spiel.

Like the others, he didn't ask any exact questions at first. He didn't say anything that related to any of us as an individual, as a person. That type of thing they evidently do with the office workers, because they have more time, there are fewer of them. But we were a mass, a great tide. It wasn't just two thousand, there were twenty thousand new hires. The monsters were coming, the horrible workers. They'd been at it for two months, asking everyone the same questions, the same work.

65

It pissed them off, too, the people who had to do this work. This mass of workers who were coming into Fiat had proletarianised those office workers, those doctors. It wasn't about selection; it served simply to promote a concept of organisation, of subordination, of discipline. In fact, if not, they wouldn't have taken guys who couldn't see, who really were in fact sick, who had a belly this big. They took them all, because they needed them all. Everyone was good for that kind of work.

And this guy, the chief engineer, says: I am your colonel. You're my men, and we have to respect one another. I have always defended my workers. Fiat workers are the best, the most productive, and all this bullshit. It was all getting up my nose and I was thinking: You know, this is going to end badly, me and this colonel. Then he explained that we shouldn't get involved in sabotaging production because as well as getting fired we could be reported to the police. He read out an article from the penal code that said you could be charged. You were turning yourself into a terrorist. And I started to think: a nice lesson would do this colonel good.

Then they introduced us to our foremen. They'd divided us up. We had been a mass up to that moment, then they divided us, four or five to every line. I was going to the 500 line, so they introduced my boss to me, the line foreman. Then my boss introduced the leading hand to me. The leading hand is the worker who knows how to do all the tasks on the line. If you have to go for a piss or a shit, when they let you go — because you need permission — he steps in and substitutes for you. Or if you feel sick, or get something wrong. The leading hand steps in, the joker, the guy who can do everything.

They introduced these guys to me and they got me beside the line. There was two hours of work left and the line boss got me to do some little jobs, meaningless tasks. Looking at the assembly line, it seemed like light work. How this line ran, all these workers, how they worked. It seemed like there almost wasn't any effort. The next day they took me to my station, another station on another line. And they introduced me to another line boss the next day when I had to start work. This guy gets a leading hand and tells him: Take him over there. Anyway I was at a station where I put the piece with the fenders on the Fiat 500. I had to place it in front of the engine, put two bolts on and tighten it with this thing.

I grabbed this part with the fenders; above me was the body of a 500 coming along, the engine was coming in from somewhere else, I placed this part with the fenders, which weighed around ten kilos. I got it from another station where someone else made it up, I put it over the engine, put the bolts on. I tightened it with this pneumatic driver, quick, trrr trrr two bolts, and the whole thing went off as another one arrived. Twenty seconds I had. I had to get the rhythm. The first few days I couldn't keep up and the leading hand helped me. For three days he helped me.

On the Fiat line it's not a question of learning but of getting your muscles used to it, of getting used to the force of those movements and the rhythm. Having to place a whatchamacallit every twenty seconds meant you had movements quicker than a heartbeat. That is a finger, your eye, any part was forced to move in tenths of a second: forced actions in fractions of a second. The action of choosing the two washers, the action of choosing the two bolts, those movements were actions your muscles and your eyes had to make by themselves, without you deciding anything. I just had to keep up the rhythm of all those movements, repeated in order and equally. Without three or four days to get used to the rhythm, you couldn't do it.

As I started to get used to doing it on my own the guy helping left me. I knew it was in their interests to speed up the operations. Lots of newly arrived workers only did half a day, a day, three days, some a week's work, then left. Especially a lot of the young ones, after seeing what shitty work it was. Who the fuck would want to stay here, and they took off. Then a load of others went on sick leave every day. So given there were fewer workers on the line, they needed each of us to do a lot more processes. Because if not, they would have had to keep a lot of the personnel on who weren't any use because they were never there. They stuck me with an extra process.

So I started to get pissed off and I hurt one of my fingers a bit.

I crushed my nail, but not so that I hurt myself too much. I put grease on my finger so it looked all black with dried blood. My nail was black, my finger was black and I called the leading hand and told him that I had to go to the infirmary. The line boss comes and he says: You want to go to the infirmary? Yeah, I've hurt my finger. No, you can't go to the infirmary for a finger like that. Well, I'm going. You're not going. Another supervisor arrives, the head of the 500. I mean, there's the head of the body plant, then there's the head of the 500, a head of the 850, a head of the 124. And whether it's the 124 or the 500 or the 850, they all have several lines. The 850 has three or four lines, the 500 has six or seven lines, the 124 has two or three lines.

The head of the 500 arrives and he says to me: Listen, I'll make you a proposal. You choose whether you go to the doctor, whether you go to the infirmary with that finger, or whether you want to stay here. If you want to stay here I'll give you a lighter job. If you want to go to the doctor and the doctor doesn't admit you I'll put you onto the heaviest job there is; in fact, I'll suspend you from work. So I accepted the challenge and said: I want to go to the doctor. He writes me out the slip, because you have to have a slip from him to go up to the infirmary. He warns me: Now we'll see. And I went to the infirmary. Going into the infirmary I saw a worker coming back who had one arm bandaged who'd cut himself. Are you going home? I say to him. No, they haven't admitted me. What, with that cut arm they haven't admitted you? No.

Right away I got pissed off and I said to myself: Then with this finger, even if it's nothing, I'll get them to give me ten days off. Because the guy had really hurt himself and they tell him: No, you have to work. What, are we crazy, is it war, are we in Vietnam here? With all these bloodied, injured people who absolutely have to work? I went into the infirmary and some other injured workers arrived. The infirmary was full all the time, it really seemed like a field hospital, with all these workers coming constantly, with a crushed hand, with a cut somewhere, with something broken. A guy who had a hernia came in yelling with pain. They took him to the first aid station and called an ambulance.

I turned up and started the bluff. I checked it all out, touching my finger so I knew when I had to yell. When they touched my finger I started to swear in Neapolitan dialect. The guy who was treating me was from Torino and it had a real effect on him. If I swore in Italian it would seem like I was acting, but swearing in Neapolitan, the guy didn't know if I was acting or not. Mannaggia 'a maronna, me stai cacando 'o cazzo, statte fermo porco dio,[13] that kind of thing. But I have to check you, the guy said. Hold still, please. What do you mean hold still. I've hurt my finger, here, it's broken. And he goes: I want to

70

see if it's broken, I don't know if it is broken. But I know, I can feel it's broken. I can't move it at all.

A doctor comes in, the one who had looked at the other guy's hernia: All right, give him a slip, six days. Six days, he says, then if it's still bad we'll send him to hospital. He gives me the slip and I get out of there. I go to the head and say: He gave me six days. The guy goes black with rage, thinking: This dickhead has screwed me, he'll have six days off on Fiat. It was MALF[14] that had to pay me. It wasn't the scheme that we have now, INAM.[15] MALF, Fiat's own insurance scheme, paid more. INAM didn't pay for the first three days off sick, but with MALF you were paid from the first day. It was a nice scam with Fiat having that scheme, which they dropped later.

So I took myself off home. At home I didn't wash my finger at all, with the grease making it all black. I didn't wash it and I didn't even move it, I was careful not to rest it anywhere. After six days it was all swollen. I hadn't used my finger at all, just to make it swell up. If you use your fingers, they get thin. But if you get a knock on a finger and then you don't use it at all, it really swells up and gets fatter than the others. Well, it's not as if it swells a lot, but you can see that it's a little fatter. And it's smoother, because you haven't touched anything with it.

I go back in after six days and I say: Look, this finger has really swollen up. It feels like it's still injured. But can't you work? No, because we work with our hands. If I have to grab a bolt or grab the pistol, the thing that tightens the bolts, which is called a pistol, I have to use my hands. So either I pay attention to what I'm doing, to the bolts that I'm grabbing, or I pay attention to the finger to make sure I don't knock it against anything. I'd have to pay attention to what I'm doing and to my finger, and I can't do that. After three hours of furiously knocking things against things I'll end up a nervous wreck, I'll go crazy, I'll throw something at someone's head. I can't do it.

The doctor figured that I was bluffing and he made me a proposal: Would you rather go back to work or would you rather I sent you to recover in hospital? I said to myself: Now I'll have to be hard, because a spell in hospital will cost them more. He can't justify sending a worker to hospital for a sore finger; he can't do it. He wanted to call my bluff, he was thinking: This guy wants another three or four days' holiday and so I'll threaten him. Instead of going to hospital he'll want to go back to the factory. Clearly, in hospital you're fucked, it's no fun, you're in there and that's it.

I go: No, then I'll go to hospital, because I think the finger is still injured, it hasn't healed. Then he says to someone: Give this one here the paperwork for hospital. With a sick feeling, I thought: This dickhead has screwed me. I shut up, I almost wanted to say: I'll go and work. I stretch over to have a look at the paperwork, and see that the guy was giving me another six days. I don't say a thing, I take the papers and go. Him silent, me silent. Me without saying: So I don't have to go to hospital. We both knew we were trying to take the piss out of each other.

So I got twelve days paid sick leave and I was happy. Because I'd managed to cheat the system and get something for myself. But I didn't know what the fuck to do all day with all that time on my hands. I hung around Valentino, where the hookers and fags are. I was dicking around, bored, and I didn't know what to do, even though I had money. They paid me nearly one hundred and twenty thousand lire a month at Fiat. Every fifteen days they gave you an advance, and when I got the advance I gave forty thousand to my sister, where I was staying.

I'd have ten thousand lire left, and I'd blow it in a few days. Partly because I didn't know what the fuck to do, I went from one bar to the next, bought magazines like Playmen or Diabolik. I went to the movies; I didn't know what the fuck to do. I went through that money without knowing what the fuck I was doing. I was like that, resting up, tired out by that shit work. It's a crazy thing, really absurd. In those twelve days sick leave I realised that I didn't even know how to relax away from work, and that I didn't know what the fuck to do in Torino.

At the end of the twelve days scammed from Fiat because there was fuck-all wrong with me, I go back in. They get me bolting on mufflers, and I decided to fuck with my new leading hand. When you have to learn a new process you have the leading hand there teaching you. And I wanted to fuck this guy up because the leading hands are scabs, people who've been working there for years. He showed me: See, trrr trrr trrr, you do the next one. I go: trrrrrrr and then I get stuck. I pretended to get stuck with the electric driver, I made out it was jammed on the bolt. Hurry up, I said to the leading hand, come and have a look. I can't do it.

For fuck's sake, what the fuck, goes the guy, who was from Torino. They call them 'barott'; they're from the outskirts of Torino, from peasant background. They're still really farmers, they've got land that their wives work. They're commuters, really hard people, a bit dense, lacking in imagination, dangerous. Not fascists, just really thick. They were PCI (Italian Communist Party), bread and work. As a qualunquista, I could be salvaged. But these types accepted work deep down, work was everything to them, everything, and they showed you that in their behaviour. They stayed there for years, three years, ten years, they got old quickly and died early. For a few lire, never enough, only the most insensitive type, only a drone could spend years in this shitty prison and do a job that destroys your life.

Anyway, this guy suspected that I wanted to fuck with him, and he leaves his post and stops the line. The section heads turn up. When the line stops there's a red light where it's stopped and all the bosses turn up. What's happening? This guy here doesn't want to work. Now that's a lie because I am working, I can't do it because I'm learning. It's not as if I'm smart like you, you've been here for ten years, obviously someone like you learns everything quickly. I really wanted to kill him: You're intelligent, I told him, you've been here for ten years and you understand everything, for me it's a little harder. And I'm coming back from sick leave, with this finger, how can I manage?

So the boss says to me: Listen, it looks to me like you want to slack off. But you need to get into your head that at Fiat you have to work, you can't slack off. If you want to slack off, get down to Via Roma[16] where your mates are. I tell him: Look, I don't know about mates in Via Roma. But I'm here because I need money. I'm working; I just haven't got it yet. When I get it I'll work. Are you going to give me the six days' trial or not? What do you mean six days, you've already been here for a month. Yes, a month, but I was on another line, not this one. Now I need another six days trial and the leading hand has to stay here with me for six days. Otherwise, I'm not lifting a fucking finger.

I had to tighten the bolts on the muffler, nine bolts. I had to stand there for eight hours with the driver, a pistol-type thing, the engine comes, I tighten, it keeps going. Another guy fitted the muffler and slipped the bolts in, I only had to tighten them. It was pretty easy, but I had to stand there for eight hours with the pistol in my hands or on my shoulder, a pneumatic pistol that weighed fourteen kilos. What's more, I don't like jobs where I have to use only one hand or one arm, where I don't use both together. They make one shoulder bigger, one smaller. You get all twisted, one shoulder one way and the other another way, one muscle bigger and one smaller. It really deforms you. But if you do things like gymnastics, you have to move everything at the same time, that doesn't bother me. This gymnastics on the other hand pissed me off. The motor was on my shoulder, and then there was the noise: totototoo to tot to, I couldn't handle it.

Anyway, I'd already decided to leave Fiat and make some trouble for them. At the latest confrontation with my leading hand the foremen all turned up together again. The other workers stopped because my leading hand had stopped the line. They were all there looking at me, me looking at the bosses. And I threaten them all, the boss, the leading hand, the big boss who had come down as well, the colonel. Look, I say, you need to understand that Fiat isn't me, get it into your heads. I didn't want Fiat, I didn't make it, I'm inside here just to make money and that's it. But if you piss me off and break my balls I'll smash your heads in, all of you. I told them in front of the other workers. I clearly threatened them, but they couldn't chance it, because they didn't know what I really thought, if I was being serious or not. So the big boss came over all paternal.

You're right, he says to me in front of the workers. But work is important, work is something that you have to do. It's obvious you are a little stressed today, but we can't help with that, this isn't a hospital. Go and get better, he says coming nearer to me, take some sick leave, he comes right up to me in front of the other workers, but don't hassle people who want to work. In other words, he brought me back, he brought me back and ended the discussion: If you want to break people's balls, take some sick leave, fuck off out of here, but don't hassle people who want to work and who will work. There's no place here for slackers, crazies, sick people who don't like work. So anyway, the line started up again and the workers weren't looking at me any more.

Fifth chapter **The struggle**

All of this happened before I met the comrades at the gates. One evening I was coming out of Fiat and I see a student who goes: Do you want to come to a meeting at the bar? It sounded OK to me and I told him OK, I'll go. What the fuck, I didn't have anything to do, it was OK to see what these assholes want, what they say. I saw these students every day, and I figured they were assholes. I didn't know what they were talking about, I never read their leaflets.

There were strikes at the time organised by the union. It was the workers who wanted promotion to second category, the crane operators and forklift divers. There were strikes inside; some lines, the 124 lines, had stopped. The workers were playing cards for money. They were reading or sitting around because the parts weren't coming through. Two or three lines had stopped. When I came out I saw these students handing out leaflets and talking about the strike. But I didn't care about that stuff.

Anyway I go to the meeting at the bar near Mirafiori. I meet Mario and some other students, and I tell him which workshop I'm in, what I do. I also meet some other workers and Raffaele, from the 124 line, who I had seen going to the meetings every evening. He said he knew about eighty comrades who were ready to stop work when he said. Fuck, I said to myself, I know everybody but no one is prepared to stop work when I say so. All right then, I said to him, if you know eighty comrades we can stop work when we want. We can even stop tomorrow. We won't work any more, we'll start the struggle tomorrow.

Mario and the other students were all ears hearing what this guy Raffaele and I were saying. Then it was decided to make a leaflet for the next day calling on workers to start the struggle, to go on strike. I don't know what the leaflet was supposed to mean. Something about second category, I don't know. I seem to remember that we wanted a meal allowance. At Fiat there's no cafeteria and we wanted the meal allowance they'd promised us. It would have been something like that.

Like in lots of factories, at Fiat we brought our food in lunch boxes. And I said they should pay us for the half-hour when we ate because we worked in that half-hour, too. Because the siren sounded while you were working, rrrhhh, and then you had to run off, take the stairs, get to your corridor, get to your locker room, get to your locker, grab your fork, your spoon, your bread, run, get to where your lunchbox was and there were two thousand, grab your lunchbox, get to the table, talk, tatatatatatatatatata, eat, down, uuuhhh, jump up, scramble, corridor, locker room, locker, put your stuff back, run down, half an hour, there you are again back in the workshop. All on the run, while you were going and while you were coming back to the workshop, if you didn't you couldn't make it. That's work, no way it's a break. It's productive.

So I was listening to Raffaele, who said he could bring eighty comrades out. And I told him that we should meet up tomorrow, him with his followers and me with mine. Though I didn't have any followers, I thought: we'll see if they follow me, I'll have a go. I'll see you with our guys, I say to Raffaele. Let's meet up at the end of the line and we'll have a rally. And we'll threaten all the pimps and scabs and leading hands with death, string 'em up. We'll threaten them and have a rally, with chanting and singing. Let's see what the fuck we can start, then we'll leave the workshop. In other words, let's fight, no work tomorrow. OK, OK. Then let's make this leaflet, tomorrow at one o'clock we hand them out at the gate. Then when we're inside we talk to the comrades in the locker rooms and on the way into the locker rooms.

The next day we started handing out the leaflets at the gate with the students. Mario had made a sign, I don't know what was written on it, power to the workers, the working class is strong, that kind of thing. So I started stirring things up at the gates. Comrades, today we must stop work. Because we've fucking had it up to here with work. You've seen how tough work is. You've seen how heavy it is. You've seen that it's bad for you. They'd made you believe that Fiat was the promised land, California, that we're saved.

81

I've done all kinds of work, bricklayer, dishwasher, loading and unloading. I've done it all, but the most disgusting is Fiat. When I came to Fiat I believed I'd be saved. This myth of Fiat, of work at Fiat. In reality it's shit, like all work, in fact it's worse. Every day here they speed up the line. A lot of work and not much money. Here, little by little, you die without noticing. Which means that it is work that is shit, all jobs are shit. There's no work that is OK, it is work itself that is shit. Here, today, if we want to get ahead, we can't get ahead by working more. Only by the struggle, not by working more, that's the only way we can make things better. Kick back, today we're having a holiday. I spoke in dialect because they were all Neapolitans, southerners. So that they would all understand, the official language there was Neapolitan.

Then we went inside, and while we were going in I had an idea. I got Mario to give me the sign, I don't even know what the fuck was written on it exactly. I had a little flash of imagination, now I'm going into Fiat with a sign. I'm going in with a sign in one hand, my ID card in the other. Because to get in you have to show your ID card, whether you're an employee or not. If not who knows, a thief could get in, someone with a bomb. The first security guard looks at me all surprised, mouth open. It's the first time in his life he has seen a placard inside Fiat, passing the gate legally, with Fiat ID card in hand. The head security guard comes up to me and says: Stop, please. Are you talking to me? Yes, what are you doing with that sign?

I go, With this? I hold it out. You know you can't come in with a sign. And where is that written down? There's nothing in the regulations about not entering with signs, so I'm going in. No, you can't enter. But you're making that up, you're just saying that I can't enter, but I'm going in. I like this sign and I'm taking it with me. No, you can't enter with things that aren't related to work. Then why is that guy going in with the Corriere dello Sport, what the fuck has the Corriere dello Sport got to do with work and workers? At least this sign concerns workers, that newspaper hasn't got anything to do with anyone. I don't give a toss, you come with me. And I say: if I leave the sign can I come in? Yes, leave the sign. Look, I'm leaving it here outside the gate. Is that OK?

I go inside. The head security guard calls me again: You, come with me please. Where? I have to go to work. Come with me. So I grab him by the tie and I tell him: No, you come with me. I drag him along, then I give him a kick in the balls, a kick in the guts and I push him to the ground. I say: don't fuck with me, it's time for the struggle, and you can all go and get fucked. All the workers who were going in gave a rumbling roar, uhhhhh, like an Arab tribe, all of them cheering me on. Then they say: quick, inside, or they'll single you out. I run inside and go to my locker room: Comrades, it's time for the struggle, let's go and turn the place upside down.

They all went white. It was too provocative. They had never been in a struggle. The union never showed up there. They were thinking: where did this guy come from, this nut who says we have to take up the struggle. Anyway, I was waiting for them at the bottom of the stairs. Today, the struggle must start. But how? We go down, and instead of going to the lines we make one big group down at the end of the lines. But these guys didn't go. They were frustrated, stuck, they didn't understand, they all went to the lines. They all had the neurosis.

What is the neurosis? Every Fiat worker has a gate number, a corridor number, a locker room number, a locker number, a workshop number, a line number, a number for the tasks they have to do, a number for the parts of the car they have to make. In other words, it's all numbers, your day at Fiat is divided up, organised by this series of numbers that you see and by others that you don't see. By a series of numbered and obligatory things. Being inside there means that as you enter the gate you have to go like this with a numbered ID card, then you have to take that numbered staircase turning to the right, then that numbered corridor. And so on.

In the cafeteria for example. The workers automatically choose a place to sit, and those remain their places for ever. It's not as if the cafeteria is organised so that everyone has to sit in the same place all the time. But in fact you always end up sitting in the same place. It's like, this is a scientific fact, it's strange.

I always ate in the same seat, at the same table, with the same people, without anyone ever having put us together. Well this signifies neurosis, according to me. I don't know if you can say neurosis for this, if it is the exact word. But to be inside there you have to do this, because if you don't do it you can't stay.

These guys I'd talked to about the struggle couldn't accept it, they didn't know what the fuck to do. They didn't understand what I was proposing. They felt somehow that what I was proposing was right, but they didn't know how to act on it. They didn't understand that the important thing was to stir things up all together. I got pissed off. Not because I would get fired for what I had done, because they already wanted to fire me anyway, they were just looking for an excuse. I'd been at Fiat for three months and I couldn't stand it any more. I couldn't hack it any more as an employee, as a worker. It was May, it was already warming up and I wanted to go back down south and go to the beach.

I didn't get pissed off because I was going to get fired. That was certain, but I didn't give a shit about that. They could easily pick me out as I was. I had a moustache, I wore white shoes and a blue shirt, blue pants, it was easy to pick me out. And I stayed how I was when I entered the workshop, without getting changed, without taking my old shoes, my old pants, my old pullover out of my locker, without getting changed the way you always did. I'd gone in wearing what I wore out in the street, with polished white shoes, everything spot-on. I had gone into the workshop like that, committed to not working. But I was pissed off because I hadn't managed to convince the others.

I feel like getting a Coke from the machine and I drink it and arrive late to the assembly line. You always have to arrive before the line starts, never after. I found my foreman, and the other foreman, already there, and everyone looking at me. And the leading hand was at my post. I get there and the boss says: Look, you're breaking everybody's balls. You have to come on time; I'm giving you a half-hour penalty. I tell him: Do whatever the fuck you want, you're really breaking my balls, you and Fiat. Go get fucked before I fling something at your head. You can stick these filthy fucking machines, I don't give a shit.

All the workers who were standing around were looking at me and I said to them: You're a bunch of assholes, you're just slaves. You should be getting into these guards here, these fascists. What the fuck are these insects, let's spit in their faces, let's do whatever we want, this is like military service. Outside we have to pay if we go into a bar, we have to pay on the tram, we have to pay for a pensione or a hotel, we have to pay for everything.

And inside here they want to tell us what to do. For a few useless pennies, good for fuck-all, for work that kills us and that's it. We're crazy. This is a life of shit, people in prison are freer than us, chained to these disgusting machines so that we can't even move, with the screws all around us. The only thing missing is a whipping.

Anyway I started to work, reluctantly, because I wanted to fight. I wanted to do something, staying there wasn't for me. While I was there I heard shouting in the distance. The body workshops are huge sheds, so big you can't see to the end, there's a constant noise and you can't hear human speech. The workers have to shout to be heard. I heard trouble, shouting, and I said to myself: It's the comrades starting a demonstration. I didn't know where it was, you couldn't see. I abandon my post, cross all the lines, I cut across them, where all the other machines are, and I go to the comrades. I get there and I join in the shouting, too. We were shouting the strangest things, things that had fuck-all to do with anything, to create a moment of rupture: Mao Tsetung, Ho Chi Minh, Potere operaio.[17] Things that had no connection to anything there but that we liked the sound of.

Things like Long Live Gigi Riva, Long Live Cagliari,[18] Long Live Pussy we shouted. We wanted to shout things that had nothing to do with Fiat, with all that we had to do in there. So everyone, people who had no idea who Mao or Ho Chi Minh was, were shouting Mao and Ho Chi Minh. Because it had fuck-all to do with Fiat, it was OK. And we started to organise a march, there were about eighty of us. And one by one as the march passed through the lines people joined on at the back. We found some cartons and tore them up and wrote on them with chalk: Comrades leave the lines your place is with us. On another one we wrote: Potere operaio. On yet another: To arselickers work, to workers the struggle. And we went marching on with these signs.

The march got bigger and the union officials arrived. It was the first time in my life I had seen union officials inside Fiat. The officials start up: Comrades, there's no need to fight now. We'll take up the struggle in autumn with the rest of the working class, with all the other metalworkers. Now means weakening the struggle, if we fight now how will we fight in October? We tell them: We need to fight now because it's still spring and the summer is ahead of us. In October we'll need overcoats and shoes, we'll need to pay for the central heating in our apartments, schoolbooks for our children. So the worker can't fight in autumn, he has to fight in summer. In summer he can sleep in the open air if he has to, but not in winter. And you know that Fiat needs more product in spring, if we stop now we'll mess up Fiat, but in October they won't give a shit.

The union officials got us into little groups, to divide us up, to break up the march. About twenty of us start another march somewhere else and get some comrades back. In two hours we manage to stop all the lines. Right at that moment the boss of the body plant arrived, the colonel. We were in workshop 54, but all the lines had stopped because we'd gone into the other workshops and we'd made them all stop. The colonel arrives, and as he comes a space opens up among the workers, everyone suddenly goes back to the lines. Fifteen of us were left alone there with signs. So I decide that this is the right moment to confront him, because if not we were pissing everything away.

He comes towards us and I go towards him with the sign right in his face. I plant it half a metre from his nose and he reads it. I don't remember which sign it was, something was written on it, I didn't care what. The only thing I cared about was for him to go get fucked. Make him understand that he couldn't do anything to us. He sees that I wasn't going anywhere, that I'd planted myself right there in front of him, and he says: So what are all these signs? Price tags for vegetables? Is this the market? No, I say, they're signs against the bosses, that's why we made them. Then he gets a little group of people together, the engineer of the body plant with the other workers. And around the engineer were five hundred workers who kept nodding yes, yes. He spoke and they nodded yes. The union officials gathered other groups on the other body plant lines, and we were left in a little group of fifteen isolated comrades.

So I say: Comrades, we need to act because if we don't they'll isolate us, they'll screw us. We have to intervene where the engineer is speaking because he's the biggest fish. If we can fuck up the engineer in front of the workers, we'll save everything. If we can smash the capitalistic management of this little group we're there, we've won the struggle here today. We went over to them, the engineer was speaking and I say: Can I join this discussion too? He goes: Please, speak. What do you have to say? I have only one thing to say: What productivity bonus do you get? That's none of your business, goes the engineer.

No, in fact it is my business. It's my business because the maximum productivity bonus we get ... I don't even know how much I get. I never look at what's on my pay slip, my base salary, piece rates, insurance and all of that. I just take the money, without reading it, because I'm not interested in reading it, I'm only interested in the money. But for sure we'd get five or six per cent at the most, maybe seven per cent. But how much do you get? It's none of your business. In respect of the tiny percentage that we get, I continued, you, according to the annual production of automobiles, which we make, get a bonus of millions of lire. That's why it's in your interests to make us more and more productive. While for us, the work and the money never change. Is that true or not?

I repeat, it's none of your business. How is it not my business? With my work you make millions and then you say it's none of my business. You make money because the productivity bonus increases with increases in your category. Whether you're a leading hand, a foreman, a big boss, Agnelli. The biggest bonus, clearly, is Agnelli's. I turned towards the workers: Do you know how much money this guy takes in production bonuses? Do you know why he doesn't want to tell me?

Then the colonel steps in and says: But don't you know that I've studied? That I'm an engineer? No, I don't know that, I answer. And I say: But do you know that we don't give a shit whether you've studied? That we don't recognise any authority over us other than our own any more? He says: Didn't your parents teach you anything? No, they didn't, did yours? Yes, mine did. And then he says, Have you done your military service? No, I haven't done my military service, why, what's my family and my military service got to do with it? What it has to do with it is that your family should teach you how to behave, to respect people who are more educated. And if you had done military service you would understand that there is always a hierarchy that must be respected. Whoever doesn't respect this hierarchy is an anarchist, a criminal, crazy.

You could say that I'm crazy, but there is also the fact that I don't like work. There, there it is, he shouts, you've all heard it, all of you, people who strike don't like work. And so, I say, why do these guys prefer standing and talking to you over getting onto the lines? You can see that none of these people like work either. Anything, any excuse is enough, even standing and listening to someone talk. Workers don't like work, workers are forced to work. I'm not here at Fiat because I like Fiat, because there isn't a single fucking thing about Fiat that I like, I don't like the cars that we make, I don't like the foremen, I don't like you. I'm here at Fiat because I need money.

As I see it you won't be here for much longer, the colonel says. I hear that a security guard was beaten up outside. If I find out who did it, I will make him pay dearly. You don't have to go far to find out who it was, I say. I've never liked riddles very much. I know you'll make me pay, but I really don't give a shit. I gave that guy a beating and I'll give someone else a beating tonight. The guy caught the sniff of a beating and got himself out from among us workers quick smart. The fifteen of us had lined up in front of him, and behind him were all the other workers. He runs off, but first he says to me: What is your name? I tell him my name, my surname, the name of my foreman, that I'm in workshop 54, on the 500 line, and that I'm always available. I tell him all this to show that I'm not afraid of him. You'll see, I'll make you pay. Ah, get fucked, get out of here you fucking prick, you'll make me pay some other time.

He goes off, and as he goes all the workers: ehhhhhhhhhh, a shout, everybody cheering: You're a legend, you fucked him up all right, that guy's a real prick, he wanted to make fools out of us. OK, OK, I say, we've done that, but now it's time to march. We have to fuck things up for good, smash everything in here now. And we kicked our boots against the cartons of supplies, making a sullen, violent noise, dududu dududu, a couple of hours of this uproar. Now and again we'd have a sort of meeting, one time at the north end of the lines, then at the south. We wound our way through them shouting all together: More money less work. Vogliamo tutto: we want everything. We climbed up and down the lines and held more meetings.

On like that until the evening. When evening came I went to punch my time card. My time card wasn't there, they'd taken it away. I go to the supervisor. Boss, where's my time card? He says: Isn't it there? Don't mess around, where have you put it? I reply. I don't know where it is, he goes, if it's not there it means you'll have to wait and then we'll see. OK, I'll wait then. Anyway, all the workers head off, they all leave. It was just me, it seemed, at Mirafiori. While I wait another foreman turns up, then another, and another. I say to myself: Hey, this smells like security guards. Boss, where's my time card? You have to come to the office, he goes.

Like fuck I'm coming to the office. I'm coming into the factory again tomorrow, with or without my time card. But I'm not coming to the office. If the colonel has something to say to me he can come and say it here in the workshop. I haven't got anything to say to him, it's him who wants to say something to me. And I took off quickly so I wouldn't be the last one there. Some workers were coming out of the locker rooms where they'd showered and dressed. I catch up with my work-mates and say: Comrades, they want to grab me and report me. They'll grab me at the gate and slip some bit of junk into my pocket and call the police and report me for theft. That's how they do it.

All arranged. They'd grab me, put any old bit of metal in my pocket, a bolt or a spanner. They'd call the police: we caught him stealing, and this morning he beat up a security guard. They'd give me three years. This was their scheme. They wanted to get me at any cost. I went ahead with the com-rades. Let's stay on our toes at the gate. Because at the gate a guard picks you out, makes you go into a room and pokes around in your bag and your clothes. If they pick me out now, I say to the comrades, I'm not going in for the search, because if I go in I'm fucked. We go on, we get to the gate and I see the foreman, my foreman, surrounded by guards, five of them. The foreman goes: It's him, that one there.

A guard comes forward, he'd be the head-kicker in this sit-uation, and says: You, actually, You, please, because they're always formal at Fiat, You, please, come with me. Who, me? Why do I have to come? Come with me please. I don't want to come. Please come with me. I don't want to come, what do you want with me? Why, have you never been searched before? Yes, but this afternoon I don't feel like it, and I haven't got a bag, look, I'm wearing a pullover. I lifted it to show my bare chest. I'm wearing pants, that's all, I haven't got anything on me, can't you see? Ciao. Come here, he yells.

He grabs me around the neck, this fucking goon, and drags me along. So I think about what the fuck to do for a moment. I pretend to go with him. Then I put a foot in front of him and give him a shoulder in the back. Punft, he falls to the ground like a cow turd. I give him a kick in the balls. Two other guards jump me. The first one holds me by the legs and these other two on top. I kick them and elbow them and manage to throw them off. Then I'm beside them with my head down because the monster is holding me tight. At this point another comrade pulls on the arm that this asshole has around my neck like a vice. I pull his arm away, jump up, spit in the animal's face. And run. Then they grab the other comrade, and they fired him, because he helped me.

And I left. I went out and there were loads of workers and students outside. Outside the gates all the comrades were talking about the struggle. There were comrades who said I'd done the right thing by fighting the guards. That the day had been a great struggle, really satisfying. And we had a meeting right then. A huge mass of workers went to the bar, so many that you couldn't get in. And there I met Emilio and Adriano and a load of other comrades. That evening a whole lot of us decided to hold a demo at the university. And that was the beginning of the big struggle at Fiat. That was May 29, a Thursday.

Second part

Sixth chapter **The wage**

It had already been two or three weeks since it all started at Fiat. The struggles had begun after the strike for Battipaglia, which to be on the safe side the union at Fiat only held for three hours. The first political rally was on April 11, 1500 workers from the South Presses. It was the first chance Fiat workers had taken to fight against the bosses' plans, which are to create unemployment and take the people of the south by hunger. To create a massive reserve of young people and force them to work in the factories in the north. Work that became almost a prize, a gift the bosses give us. To make us come and sleep in the stations and pile into one room paying rents that were like highway robbery.

A worker explained all of this to the Maintenance workshop after the strike at Battipaglia. He climbed onto a table in the cafeteria and explained why southerners are forced to come to the north. So the management took the usual steps: transfer the worker to Mirafiori North, isolating him from everyone. But by Tuesday the 15th another group of workers are talking in a second meeting. They burst into the cafeteria, asking for a stop-work and demanding that the internal commission return the worker to his team immediately. I didn't know this had already happened then. I learnt about it later from some comrades. After I'd chucked in work there for good. After the trouble I set off that day at Mirafiori.

Over the next 48 hours Maintenance started the fight about categorisation and allowances over the minimum: two hours per shift. They demand the elimination of category three for Maintenance. To get category one workers into the struggle the union demands increases in the over-award allowances. The workers give the go-ahead to stop work straight away. The union holds back. But it's just a taste. Another month would pass before the struggle started in all Fiat's divisions.

How Mirafiori works. The first of the two big production streams starts in the Foundries, where they make motor parts, the blocks and the aluminium heads. From there to the Mechanics, where the motors are built and finished with other parts. Then the motors go into Assembly, the actual assembly line. The second stream starts in the Presses, where the body parts are stamped out of sheet metal. From here to Assembly, where they are welded together and painted. While the body shells are moving along the line, the engines and the mechanical parts are added. The vehicles are dressed, given tyres and at the end they come out into the yard.

In the middle of May the forklift drivers went on strike. To run down stocks, with the extra hit of heavy goods being held up in the workshops, because the forklift drivers loaded them onto the internal transports, the strike went for three whole shifts. At noon on the first day Fiat made its first offer: 40 lire an hour extra for all the category three forklift drivers, so as to maintain the hierarchy with the 10 lire an hour difference from category two. Offer flatly refused by the forklift drivers at Mirafiori North.

Monday May 19 the forklift drivers strike again for the whole first shift. The workers break out of their teams and get workshop meetings going. The foremen's proposal to send a delegation of workers to the management for discussions is rejected. The forklift drivers reply that they'd be more comfortable if Fiat sent its representatives to the workers' meetings. In the meetings the workers decide: The most important thing is the wage claim.

What is the worker's wage. I never read my pay packet because I didn't give a shit about it. But the things the boss divides the worker's wage into are written on the pay packet. Above all he divides it into two parts. The first part, which is the base pay, corresponds to the hours that the worker spends in the factory. This, which should be the whole wage, is actually very low, it's never enough for a worker's minimum living expenses. Then there's the other part of the wage, the so-called variable part. There can be all kinds of components in the variable part: productivity bonuses, bonuses for diligence, piecework, various loadings and so on.

All of these components tie the worker's wage to production for the boss. The piece rate, for example, is the pay for the number of units the worker produces. So that the worker has to stay on his toes and follow the foremen's orders, because they determine this variable part of his wage, which is absolutely indispensable to him for living. And this lets the boss maintain political control of the working class. To make the working class accept collaborating in their own exploitation. And this is why, when we ask for increases in our base pay, the bosses and the unions always offer increases in the variable part.

Because the more the bosses pay us this way, the more the worker's wage is tied to productivity, and the more the bosses' political control increases. Although with piecework we can get back at the bosses by autolimitation, which is when a worker makes fewer units than he should. When the worker makes more units, the boss gets more in the exchange than he gives back to the worker. But with autolimitation, the small amount of money that the worker misses out on is exchanged for many fewer units for the boss, who therefore loses out more.

This variable part of the wage is what pays for the varying amounts of labour the worker supplies. Then there's the so-called vertical structure of wages, which is the difference in wages between one worker and another depending on the kind of work he does. It's the system of grades and categories, and the other means that the bosses use to divide workers among themselves. Job allowances, merit increases, over-award payments, performance evaluation, all the way to primitive methods such as off-the-books payments and black work. All of this pays for the different quality of labour supplied by the worker.

But this idea, that the kinds of labour a worker does have different value, that he is paid more or less than another worker, is a completely capitalist invention. The bosses invented it to have another instrument of political control of the working class. Let's not forget that the Party and the unions support this capitalist invention. They accept that the money a worker gets should be based on the different quality of the work he does.

All these differences in pay function for the boss as a constant form of blackmail of the worker: if you want a grade, if you want to get ahead, you have to be good, not stir things up, not go on strike. And it's useful for dividing workers during struggles, because then everyone makes different claims according to their grading and category, and so they fight divided. And the boss can always find a helpful union official to sign off on the various increases and percentages for the different grades and categories.

Then there's the matter of working hours. Eight hours of work, if not nine or ten, that destroy the worker completely. So not much energy is left for him to communicate with other workers and organise politically. Why do the bosses want to keep working hours so long? First of all, to keep political control outside the factory as well. The question of productivity comes second. But today workers are refusing work, they want shorter working hours so they can organise themselves politically.

And finally the regulations, the division of the workforce into two sectors by the boss. Blue-collar workers on one side, clerical and technical staff on the other. For example, the regulations for sick leave are all worked out to force labour on the worker. If he is absent for three days the worker actually loses his whole wage. This doesn't happen under the clerical and technical employees' regulations. This is worked out precisely to prevent the worker staying at home when he doesn't feel like working.

But the workers' only objectives are their economic and material needs, what they need to live, and they don't give a shit about the bosses' needs, about the productivity that decides the degree to which those needs are satisfied. So it's clear that the political problem is to attack all the tools of political control that the boss holds and that he uses to bind the working class and force us to serve his productive ends and to take part in our own exploitation. The workers' weapon for fighting this tool is the refusal of the wage as compensation for the quantity and quality of work. It is therefore the refusal of the link between the wage and production. It's the demand for a wage that is no longer fixed by production for the bosses, but by the material needs of the workers. That is: Equal increases in the base wage for everyone. Material incentives such as piece rates, categories and so on are only the worker participating in his own exploitation.

And who has the pimp's job of negotiating with the bosses for a few more lire for the worker in exchange for new tools of political control? It's the union. And it then becomes itself a tool of political control over the working class. Fighting for its economic and therefore political objectives, the working class always ends up clashing with the union. Because when workers no longer want to give the boss more political control in return for an economic increase, then the union that has the pimp's role of negotiating this exchange is put out of the game by the workers.

From here therefore the working-class need for a guaranteed wage not linked to productivity. From here the working-class need for increases in base pay without waiting for contract negotiations. From here the working-class need for a 40-hour week, 36 for shift workers, paid at 48 now. From here the working-class need for parity in the awards now. For the simple act of going into the factory hell: We want a guaranteed minimum wage of 120,000 lire a month:

Because we need this money to live in this shitty society. Because we no longer want the piece rates to have us by the throat. Because we want to eliminate the divisions between workers invented by the boss. Because we want to be united so we can fight better. Because then we can more easily refuse the boss's hours. Because more money in base pay means a greater possibility of struggle. We want 40 hours, 36 for shift workers, paid at 48 now:

Because we don't want to spend half our lives in a factory. Because work is bad for you. Because we want more time to organise ourselves politically. We want the same regulations for blue-collar and white-collar workers now:

Because we want a month's holidays. Because we want to carry out the struggle against the boss as workers and technicians together. Because we want to stay at home without losing our whole wage when we just can't work any more.

Around 11.30am on Monday 19 the forklift drivers at Mirafiori North contacted the comrades at South. Half an hour later the forklift drivers at Mirafiori South stopped work until 2.30pm.

On the second shift another two-hour strike in support of the 50 lire. If they offer 50 we'll ask for 70, they say. The union schedules a forklift drivers strike for the next day, two hours per shift at the start of the shifts. The workers strike for three on the first shift and the same on the second. On Wednesday 21 the bosses end the strike in the first shift after six hours. But before the end the crane-drivers leave, stopping for two hours over the question of categories and halting resupply of parts to the assembly lines.

On Thursday May 22 the forklift and crane drivers' picket spreads to the first fixed sections. The workers from the Major Presses join the struggle. The union announces a strike of two hours per shift. The first shift's strike from 10 to 12 starts with a march in the factory that pulls workers who are still working off the machines. Fiat's attempt to make up the backlog created by these first strikes fails. In the morning the supervisors try to push the 124 line from 600 to 641 units. The workers refuse to start work. The management and the internal commission convince them to start but they have to forget about the 41 extra units.

At 2.30pm on that same Thursday 22 the second shift goes into the Major Presses but can't do much because the forklift drivers' strike is holding up the supply of parts. After an hour the two-hour strike starts as scheduled. At this point a motion to strike from 9.30pm to 11pm, when supplies for the forklift drivers would arrive, is passed. A manager comes by and asks the workers what they want, but no one wants anything. The manager concludes that they don't know. The internal commission arrives hot on the manager's heels saying that the Press workers shouldn't do what the forklift drivers are doing, striking on their own. That it hurts all of Fiat, and it could go to a lock-out.

The union officials had proposed a stop-work from three until five for the third shift. But the workers decide all together to stop from two until seven. On Friday 23 the first shift in the Presses does the two hours scheduled by the union and after discussion they decide to extend the strike until 2.30pm. Meanwhile the workers on the assembly lines take up their comrades' invitation to join the struggle. From that day no more 124s or 125s come out of Mirafiori, and only a few 600s and 850s. Almost 12,000 workers are on strike. On Saturday 24 the union decides it's not worth striking because there's only one shift. There's work, but with autolimitation of production: only 1300 units come out instead of the normal 3500.

In the meetings and discussions they say: Our aim isn't just 50 lire, even if it would make us comfortable, our aim is a permanent workers organisation that can fight the boss at every moment. Fuck democracy, there's been democracy for 25 years and for 25 years we've been getting it in the arse. We must organise ourselves, we are the unions, no army is stronger than the working class united and organised. The struggle continues in the following days, with more marches and meetings in the sections, spreading spontaneously to the Medium and Small Presses. Here the workers call the strikes autonomously, not the union. Why does this strike go on for days and days and spread like wildfire? What do the workers of Fiat want?

For the first time the workers of Fiat aren't acting for particular claims made by the union, such as for the line delegate. Instead they refuse en masse the organisation of work in the factory, deciding for themselves. For 80, 90, 100 thousand lire a month they work at a murderous rate, unbearable, which the boss increases constantly. In fact in the 124 body workshop they made 320 vehicles a day at the beginning of 1968, 360 in October, 380 after Avola.[19] Now the bosses are pushing for 430 and are only accepting less because of the struggle. These increases are only possible through the acceleration of the assembly line. But the workers of Fiat don't want to know any more about it, they want to decide for themselves how much they work.

They all want a guaranteed wage that will let them live and they don't give a shit about merit increases, increases in the percentage, variables etc. That is, all the mechanisms that the bosses, with the unions, have invented to tie wages more tightly to exploitation and to divide workers among themselves. They don't give a shit about the line delegate that the union wants them to fight for. The line delegate is a type of controller who has to police the agreements over work rates, that is, over the intensity of exploitation. But this is precisely what the workers are refusing. It's a struggle against the work rates that the workers want.

But now the bosses need the line delegates. They want them present at the negotiations, quick, and when the contracts are signed. They need them to assure, permanently, democratic control over the workers and their political actions. But now the workers of Fiat have decided to bring forward the fight between the bosses and the union that happens when the contracts expire. Contracts that would stop the struggle for three years and advance the bosses' plans. All of this is discussed and decided by the Fiat workers in section meetings. During working hours the workers try to build their own autonomous organisation for the first time.

What have the unions done up to now? They've tried to extinguish the struggles or to isolate them. In the Medium and Small Presses and in the Mechanical workshops they said the wildcat strike was illegal: We won't negotiate if you do it. They said that non-union strikes were sabotage. They said that if big wage increases were won they'd be absorbed into the national contract. But this isn't true because at that time new agreements were signed at Nebiolo and Olivetti that excluded absorption of the increases.

They distorted the reality of the struggle by spreading rumours, for example that the struggle at the Presses was over, but that wasn't true. Saying that if production was damaged by linking the struggles, that is, by the different sections striking for two hours and coordinating their actions to stop production, Fiat would institute a lockout.

They spread rumours that if the lines were still closed the following week Fiat would stand the workers down. They bluffed about the negotiations, saying that they'd achieved certain results, which they hadn't. They spread the idea that it was necessary to avoid recreating the atmosphere of the 1950s at Fiat, the witch hunts and sackings of the most active workers.

They said there was the risk of ending up with a separate early contract at Fiat, and so destroying unity in the sector, but that is exactly what they had always done. Workers: if the unions have continued to isolate and damp down the struggle, if all the newspapers of whichever party don't report what is really happening at Fiat, the workers' watchword must be: everybody out at Fiat. To the threats of suspension the workers of Mirafiori respond: everybody out at Fiat.

Tuesday May 27: Strike for eight hours. A march started inside the factory and wound through workshops 5, 7, 13 shouting: Potere operaio. Carrying signs that say: Less work, more pay.

The march started with a meeting of workers who had just entered the factory. During the meeting it was decided that we wanted: a rise of 50 lire for everybody plus 80 lire for the night shift on five weeks. Attack on the production schedules. The union must become the instrument for realising the workers' decisions.

Strikes called by the workers in internal assemblies: Workshop 13, first and second shift. Workshop 1, first shift 4 hours, second shift 4 hours. Workshop 3, first shift 4 hours, second shift 4 hours. Strikes called by the unions: Maintenance, first shift 2 hours, second shift 2 hours. Workshop 5, first shift 4 hours, declared at 2 hours. Second shift 8 hours, declared at 2 hours. The day's production fell to minimum levels.

Newsheet at gates 15 and 17, Press workshops: Fiat is mocking us with an offer of 7 lire. The union is mocking us by saying that Fiat is offering 36.30 lire. Let's see about this 36.30 lire. We've already got 21.50, the meal agreement from last month. 9.80 is tied to piecework so we'd have to sweat it out day by day. Plus 5, the 5 lire that the management has increased to 7 with great effort. We won't sell ourselves for 7 lire. The struggle continues. The Mechanical workshops and the lines are about to join the struggle. Newsheet at gates 18 and 20, Mechanical workshops: The struggle at the Presses and Maintenance continues. It needs to be extended to the Mechanical workshops and the lines. We must demand category two for everyone, including those on the Mechanical lines. We have to realise workers' control over the schedules and the number of cars we work on.

Newsheets on the struggle passed out at gates 1 and 2 of the lines: The strike at the Presses continues, don't believe the rumours spread by the bosses. Presses and Maintenance can't strike on their own but ask for your cooperation. Because the problems of the struggle are the same: Control over production. Advancement of category for everyone. How can we join the struggle with the Presses and Maintenance? By stopping the processes that are still functioning. Wednesday 28 May: On the body workshop lines the workers stopped, attempting a march. The section head arrived and stopped them.

Thursday 29 May: A young southern worker tried to go in with a sign. The guards stopped him and it set off a scuffle. On the second shift a group of 80 or so workers from the body workshop meet at the end of the lines straight after clocking on and march to hold up the 500 line, the only one that had kept running at full speed for the previous two days. At this point supervisors and the union intervened in a joint action that reduced the march to about 15 workers. These workers shrugged them off, they continued going about among the other workers discussing and bit by bit the march regroups, completely stopping production. Not a single car comes out of Fiat.

Seventh chapter **The comrades**

As I came out of the Fiat gate after I'd escaped the clutches of the guards, I couldn't wait to find the other comrades, either the comrades I'd been in the struggle with inside or the students who I'd made and handed out leaflets with at the entrance. I thought about things while I was heading to the bar to meet up with the comrades. Things I had thought about at other times, but this time I felt I was coming to the full conclusion.

I'd had all kinds of work in my life. Construction worker, porter, dishwasher in a restaurant, I'd been a labourer and a student, which is also a job. I'd worked at Alemagna, at Magneti Marelli, at Ideal Standard. And now I'd been at Fiat, at this Fiat that was a myth, because of all the money that they said you made there. And I had really understood something. That with work you could only live, and live poorly, as a worker, as someone who is exploited. The free time in your day is taken away, and all of your energy. You eat poorly. You are forced to get up at an impossible hour, depending on which section you're in or what work you do. I understood that work is exploitation and nothing more.

Now this myth of Fiat was ending. I'd seen that a job at Fiat was the same as a construction job, the same as washing

dishes. And I'd discovered that there was no difference between a construction worker and a metalworker, between a
metalworker and a porter, between a porter and a student.
The rules the teachers applied in those technical schools and
the rules the bosses applied in all the factories where I had
been were the same. So this posed a great problem for me.
That is, I thought, what do I do now? What do I do, what do I
have to do?

I hadn't stolen yet, I'd never had a gun. I'd never been friendly
with the so-called low-life. At least I would have had an outlet,
whether for feeling pissed-off, for my dissatisfaction, or for
my needs, my material life. I wasn't a doctor or a lawyer, a
professional. So it wasn't as if I could say, OK, I'll become a
thief or a freelancer. I was really nothing; I couldn't do a thing.

Yet I had this desire to live, to do something. Because I was
young and blood was coursing through my veins. The pressure was pretty high, in other words. I wanted to do something. I was ready for anything. But it was clear that for me
anything no longer meant worker. This was already a dirty
word. It meant almost nothing to me. It meant to keep living the shitty life I had lived up to that moment. What did
I care about work, which I had never liked and had never
cared about? And what was I supposed to make of work if it
didn't even bring me enough money to get by comfortably?
Now I understood everything, I had experimented with all the

possible ways of living. First I wanted to be inside, then I understood that inside the system I would always have to pay. For whatever kind of life, there was always a price to pay.

Whatever you want to do, if you want to buy a car or a suit, you have to work extra, you have to do overtime. You can't have a coffee or go to the movies. In a system, a world where the scope is only to work and produce goods. Anything you want to get from this system you have to put back. But really, physically, from yourself. I'd understood this. So the only way to get everything, to satisfy your needs and desires without destroying yourself, was to destroy this system of work for the bosses as it functioned. And above all to destroy it here at Fiat, in this huge factory, with so many workers. This is capital's weak link, because if Fiat stops, everything else goes into crisis, everything blows up.

I got to the bar and found lots of comrades waiting for me. We all embraced, celebrating what we'd done. All Mirafiori had stopped, even the 500 lines. Production had stopped completely on the second shift. Even though the union had shut down the struggle in Maintenance, with laughable results. One by one the others arrived, the students arrived, other workers I had never seen who had been in the struggle arrived. Everyone spoke and it was decided that the strike should continue tomorrow.

Even the workers from the big automatic lathes wanted to try to strike the next day. They decide that workers from the second shift would wait in the factory for workers from the third shift, and the third shift would wait for the first. They say they want to march in the factory to shut down other workshops. Workers from the Mechanical lines want to strike for the whole shift. There is a long discussion. It's decided to let the strike go ahead for the first shift tomorrow, from 7.30 until 11. The demands: refusal of the schedules, refusal of categories, large wage increases, the same for everyone. We want less work and more money, we write in large print on the leaflet that is made to hand out tomorrow at the gates.

And I finally had the satisfaction of discovering that the things I had thought for years, the whole time I'd worked, the things that I believed only I thought, everyone thought, and that we were really all the same. What difference was there between me and another worker? What difference could there be? Maybe he was heavier, taller or shorter, wore a different coloured suit, or I don't know what.

But the thing that wasn't different was our will, our logic, our discovery that work is the only enemy, the only sickness. It was the hate that we all felt for work and the bosses who made us do it. That's why we were all so pissed off, that's why when we weren't on strike we were all on sick leave, to escape that prison where they took away our freedom and our strength, day after day. I finally saw that what I had thought on my own for a long time was what everyone thought and said. And I saw that my own struggle against work was a struggle we could all have together and win.

Sometimes you don't understand each other and you don't agree because one person is used to thinking one way and someone else in a different way. One person like a Christian, another like a lumpenproletarian, another like a bourgeois. But in the end, in the fact of having been in a struggle together, we were able to speak the same language, to find that we all had the same needs. And these needs made us all equal in the struggle, because we all had to struggle for the same things. The meeting was fantastic, it stirred us up. Everyone recounted what had happened on the line. Because nobody could know everything that happened in that factory, where there are twenty thousand workers just in the body plant.

As if anyone could know everything that happened. The supervisors, the workers, what they said, what they did during the struggle. Recounting everything like this, we discovered a series of things. The organisation was being created, the comrades said, it's the one thing we needed to win the struggles. And as soon as a comrade spoke about what had happened on his line, how he had convinced the others to take part in a march, in the strike, in a meeting; as he explained these things, right away I found this comrade, who I had never even seen before, familiar. He became like someone I had always known. He became like a brother, I don't know how to say it. He became a comrade. You discover, here's a comrade, someone who has done the same things as me. And the only way to understand that we all think in the same way is to do the same things.

At the end of the meeting a leaflet was worked out, and how to carry on the action the next day. The comrades advised me not to go into the factory because they would arrest me. They even said I shouldn't go home because the police might come, and a comrade took me to stay at his place. And I really liked this, because it was the help we all offered each other in the struggle, it was our organisation. And in fact the next day I phoned my sister and she said the police had been there that evening looking for me. My mother wrote to me from home saying the Carabinieri were asking after me in Salerno. They went to my sister's house three or four more times.

Fiat had filed a complaint for injuries to the guard. I went to the doctor at the insurance agency and got him to give me a medical certificate for ten days because I had a scratch the guard had given me. I put myself on sick leave. Then after a week I went to get paid out, unannounced. Because I still had my Fiat ID card I could get into the factory. And as I get to my work station, on the line, my supervisor comes up to me with two guards and says: You have to come with me to the office.

I look at my line, where I was standing. There wasn't a single comrade, not one; I was alone. And I didn't know whether to put my hands up, what the fuck to do, I had no idea. I go to the office, and they make me wait there for the colonel, the Engineer. And while I'm waiting, I take the Fiat ID card from my pocket and put it right in the middle of the Engineer's desk. Because it was the Fiat ID card that they wanted, to stop me coming into the factory. After a moment the Engineer comes in and says: Ah, that's exactly what I wanted, you understand. I'm sitting there, spread out on a sofa, but he doesn't say a thing.

Another guard comes in, a huge gorilla, and goes: What are you doing sitting there? Huh. I'm sitting down because I'm tired. You have to get up. I don't feel like standing up, if you want, get me up yourself. You think you're strong, he goes, coming towards me. I don't think I'm anything, it's just I don't feel like it, it's a pain in the arse. Anyway, he says, you're lucky I wasn't outside the other night. If I'd been there I would have given you something. I know, you would have killed me, but you weren't there, so calm down. It was a fascist-type provocation, to get me into a fight, so they could give it to me and then report me, call the police and finally put me away.

I didn't fall for it, because in there I would have really copped it, they would have killed me. I signed the papers that they brought, my resignation and all that crap. And when I went out there were twenty, actually twenty, guards outside the door to the office expecting a brawl. They escort me to the locker room, I get my things, and they escort me right out of the place. A month later I went to the building where the insurance agency was with the slip to get my money. As for the complaint they filed against me, I never heard what became of it. There must have been some kind of amnesty or something.

In the morning I woke up at the house of the comrade where I'd gone to stay, then we went to the student's place. There was a meeting there with a load of comrades. The leaflet that had been mimeographed during the night was handed out and we went down to the factory. Big groups of people formed and the comrades who were going in said even they were being stopped. The workers who were going in already knew what the aims of our struggle were, the struggle for equal things for everyone that had been carried on up to then. The workers didn't value the work they did at all, they didn't feel like they were second or third category, they all felt the same, exploited. For the first time workers were fighting to all get the same pay. To have the right to the same working conditions as the clerical workers. Equal pay rises for everyone, the same category for everyone: they were excited by these things, which united them.

And that's how it was then, every day. Early in the morning we went to hand out leaflets at the gates, or the weekly newspaper of the struggle, which was called La Classe. There were all these leaflets and these newspapers from the struggle. Then you slept for a while, then you went back to the gates at one-thirty or two to hand out leaflets when the second shift went in. And you waited for the first shift to come out, for meetings with the guys from the first shift. You went again in the evening around eleven to wait for the workers from the second shift to come out and you got together with them, you had meetings. The gates of Mirafiori were like a street market in those days. Everyone was there, unionists, PCI, Marxist-Leninist kids from the Unione[20] dressed in red, police dressed in green, all competing with the hawkers who waited for the workers with fruit and vegetables, T-shirts and transistor radios. Everyone promoting their goods.

In truth the PCI, which hadn't been in the struggle, only came after July 3 to explain that the proletarians who had been beaten were just irresponsible, mercenary provocateurs. They were the same workers who the bourgeois courts later convicted. They came to explain that struggles decided and carried out by the workers autonomously were dangerous because they allow the bosses to resort to repression. They came to accuse us of being no more than little groups who were estranged from the factory, but they didn't explain how such miserable little groups could carry on a struggle as long and as powerful as the struggle of those months.

Unionists, PCI bureaucrats, fake Marxist-Leninists, cops and fascists all have one characteristic in common. They have a total fear of the workers' struggle, of the workers' ability to tell the bosses and the bosses' servants to go to hell and to organise their struggle autonomously, in the factory and outside the factory. We made them a leaflet that finished like this: Someone once said that even whales have lice. The class struggle is a whale, and cops, Party and union bureaucrats, fascists and fake revolutionaries are its lice.

Friday May 30: Whereas yesterday the strike was started by a few workers who organised a march, today 90 per cent of the 500 line workers refused to work. The strike lasts the whole shift and all production is stopped. The workers from the line make signs and organise a march. The workshop supervisor asks the workers how long they are staying on strike. The workers reply: until we put things right. A member of the internal commission rebukes the workers for paying more attention to the students than the union. He invites them to return to work at 10.30, saying that a meeting to discuss the workers' claims is in progress.

The maintenance workers struck for the whole night shift, and in the morning they marched to the 500 line. The painting cages have stopped. On the second shift a worker from the 124 line is elected to negotiate the claims, which are: schedule, promotion to second category after 6 months, money.

Today even the older workers were convinced and joined in the strike. A supervisor asked for the names of the strikers. The internal commission comes by, saying that Fiat is only prepared to negotiate if the strike ends.

In fact this strike caught the union waiting for the scheduled strikes. It meant to impose its fight for delegates on the lines in the slack period. It was only after two or three days of autonomous action and agitation that the union managed to regain some ground and declare its official strike.

News that in Grandi Motori a workshop of 400 workers has stopped. In the testing workshop at Spa Stura 400 workers stopped spontaneously. There had already been two stop works 15 days ago. At Mirafiori workshops the lathe operators have called a strike for Tuesday from 8 until 10. There have been spontaneous stop works in workshop 24. Rumours spread by the union have created divisions between the workers who support the students and those who support the union. A worker gives the news that at Fiat in Cordoba, Argentina, the workers went out on strike and the police opened fire, killing some of them. There were big clashes.

On Sunday June 1 and Monday June 2 there were meetings of workers and students all day. Tuesday 3 there's a strike for two hours at the lines. The 124 and 125 lines have run out of parts. Spray painting is halted for eight hours. The 124 preparation has been short of parts for eight days. One worker was saying that because the presses had stopped, Fiat was using spare parts that should have been sent to Germany to keep the lines going. Strikes on the 600 and 850 lines. Strike in workshop 55. No delegate elected. In preparation they went on strike, even though it wasn't official. The workers didn't understand the motivation for the union's strike. They don't care about the struggle for the line delegate. They call their own strikes in their own meetings for their own aims. They use the strikes called by the union to prolong them. When they're not on strike they limit production.

News from the gates on how the struggle is going. The Foundries have gone, completely out of the union's control. Workshop 2 stopped for 8 hours. The main objective — higher wages. The workers no longer trust any outside agent. They're claiming a rise of 200 lire and hour on the base wage. Grandi Motori workshop, via Cuneo, one section on strike since Thursday over categories and wages. Management offered 7 lire and second category. Workshop 13, Presses, 4-hour strike called by the union. A delegate was elected. There was a heated discussion. The delegate told the union officials they were a bunch of sell-outs. Gate 20, 800 workers stop work for 2 hours. Gate 13, autolimitation of production continues. Autolimitation of production is the worker's response to the line delegate, say the workers.

Gate 8, the strike continues. There are enough parts for 4 or 5 days. The unions push for work to start again. Workshop 53, strike succeeds. Delegate elected. The union tries to divide the workers, proposing control over work rates and refusing to fight for wages and categories. The bosses try to make up time. Before the line ran at 1 minute 50. Then at 1 minute 40. After the stop work it went down to 1 minute flat. The boss always controls the rate. Workshop 58, categories, work rates, pay. These are the objectives. The piecework delegate isn't worth anything. We'll reduce the rates ourselves.

All the struggles were planned in meetings at the gates when the first and second shifts came out. At the early meetings of workers and students only Mirafiori workers came. But then, gradually, as the struggle spread to other factories, to Spa Stura, to Lingotto, to Rivalta and so on, workers started coming from these other Fiat factories, too. And this fact really increased the chance of carrying the struggle forward, because every worker, every comrade contributed his own experiences and ideas. How to stop things, how to run marches, what our objectives should be and so on. What's best to block in the factory to hold things up with the least effort.

You need to say this, for example you need to ask for a one hundred and fifty lire raise on the base pay and reduction of work rates, second category for everyone and that kind of thing. For example the guys who take the finished cars off the end of the line and drive them across the yards and onto the transporters. They said: They don't pay us as drivers, which is second category. They pay us as warehouse hands, that is as third category, which is ten thousand lire less. Even though we have internal and external driver's licenses. So what do we do: instead of driving the cars we push them off the line, four of us. That's how we obstruct the lines, they have to stop, that way we stop everything.

The comrades came up with a load of ideas about how to take the struggle forward. In the meetings it was asked whether things had stopped inside, in the departments, in the various workshops. How the leaflet went, if any comrades had been suspended, if there had been any repressive measures. That is, whether they'd suspended comrades who'd taken part in the struggle or transferred them, that kind of thing. And according to how the mood of the struggle in the different workshops was, according to what information there was, we made a leaflet for the following day. If all the comrades who came out assured us that you could stop the next day, a strike was called for the next day with some objective.

The struggle went on for more than two months, a brutally spontaneous struggle. There wasn't a day when some section, some workshop, wasn't shut down. Every week, more or less, all of Fiat was shut down. They really were days of continual struggle. In fact the masthead of the leaflets that were made was Lotta Continua,[21] and really, at Fiat in Torino in those months there was a continuous struggle. We wanted to prevent work at any cost, we didn't want to work any more. We tried to send production into crisis for good. To bring the bosses to their knees and force them to come down and negotiate with us. We were fighting a battle to the end.

By now one thing was obvious in these meetings: all the workers understood that it was an important phase in the fight between us and the bosses, a decisive phase. You could feel the consciousness in the air. And the word revolution was said often in meetings. You saw comrades who were in their forties, who had families, who'd worked in Germany, who'd worked on building sites. People who'd had every kind of job, who already said that by sixty they'd be dead from work.

It's not fair, living this shitty life, the workers said in meetings, in groups at the gates. All the stuff, all the wealth that we make is ours. Enough. We can't stand it any more, we can't just be stuff too, goods to be sold. Vogliamo tutto — We want everything. All the wealth, all the power, and no work. What does work mean to us. They'd had it up to here, they wanted to fight not because of work, not because the boss is bad, but because the boss and work exist. In a word, the desire for power started to grow. It started for everyone, for workers with three or four children, unmarried workers, workers who had kids to put through school, workers who didn't have their own apartment. All our unbounded needs came out in concrete aims during the meetings. So the struggle wasn't just a struggle in the factory. Because Fiat has one hundred and fifty thousand workers. It was a huge struggle not just because it involved this great mass of workers.

Because the content of these struggles, the things the workers wanted, weren't the things that the unions said: the work rates are too high, let's lower the rates. Work is harmful, let's try to remove the harm, all this bullshit. They didn't want to be part of it any more. They discovered, the workers, that they wanted power outside. OK, in the factory we manage to fight, to hold up production when we want. But outside what do we do. Outside we have to pay rent, we have to eat. We have all of these needs. They discovered that they didn't have any power, the State fucked them over at every level. Outside the factory they didn't become citizens like all the other workers when they took off their overalls. They were another race. In this system of continuous exploitation they were workers outside as well. To live as workers outside too, to be exploited as workers outside too.

These leaflets that were made, which came out of the meetings, the workers took these leaflets home. Showed them to friends who worked on building sites or other places, and so they ended up all over the place. They often went to distribute them in the neighbourhoods, too, like at Nichelino: in fact, at Nichelino there was an occupation of the town hall over housing that went on for quite a few days. They said the rents were too high, they couldn't afford them. A leaflet was made that said: Rent — theft of salary. And they didn't pay any more. Some comrades from the PCI took part in the occupation, and then they left, after which the PCI did everything it could to disrupt the occupation of the town hall.

Nichelino is a working-class dormitory on the outskirts of Torino. Out of 15,000 people, 12,000 are workers, of whom 1700 work in Nichelino, 5500 at Fiat in the various plants at Carmagnola, Rivalta, Mirafiori, Airasca, Spa Stura and so on, the others in factories spread mostly throughout the Fiat cycle, for example Aspera Frigo, Carello and lots of others spread all over.

Around there a family's budget was the following: wages at a factory in Nichelino for 8 hours work varied between 60,000 and 80,000 a month. Rent — don't even think about 10,000 — varies from 20,000 to 35,000, plus 2,000, maybe 4,000 costs and central heating. That leaves between 30,000 and 50,000 for living, so that working hours have to rise to 10 or 14. Someone who works at Fiat will never get ahead at all. The cost of travel and the unpaid commuting time, at least two hours a day, uses up the rest.

Characteristics of the dwellings at Nichelino: More or less complete absence of services. Rents continually rising. Constant blackmail by the landlords, with the threat of eviction. Real difficulty for big families, particularly from the south, finding housing. During the 13-day occupation of the town hall, flyers posted on the walls told day by day of the development of the struggle at Fiat and brought the whole population into the discussion at the occupied town hall. Committees of struggle were formed in more factories with claims the same as at Mirafiori. The problems of the factory were connected to the problems outside the factory, the objectives unified the struggles.

These concrete material objectives of the struggle got right around the city, because they were things that concerned everybody, that touched everyone directly. This is what caused the explosion on July 3, the huge battle between the proletariat and the State and its police gangs. That great battle, July 3, is easily explained, because everybody on the streets and in the neighbourhoods understood immediately why those workers were demonstrating, why they were fighting the police. They weren't demonstrating just because they were radicals and had to have a demonstration. No, it was a fight for proletarian aims, the same as they'd been fighting for weeks inside Mirafiori and now it had spilled out onto Corso Traiano. For objectives that everyone had known about for weeks. Education, books, transport, housing, all of these things. The things that always fucked up the money you earned in the factory.

And they knew it would never be because of union strikes, because of the reforms that the unions asked for, that the State would graciously concede. And even if it did concede it would be all on its own terms. Never, with these strikes, with these reforms. Things always had to be taken, by force. Because they'd had it up to here with the State that always fucked them up and they wanted to attack it, because that was the real enemy, the one to destroy. Because they knew that they could have somewhere to live, that their needs could be satisfied, only if they swept away the State, that republic founded on forced labour, once and for all. That's how the great battle can be explained, not because people were pissed off by the heat on July 3.

Eighth chapter **Autonomy**

Thursday 5 June: At Mirafiori, while the lines stuttered back to work, the Foundry workers joined the struggle. Workers from workshop 2 continued to strike for 8 hours each shift. The struggle spread to workshops 3 and 4. The workers from those workshops decided to join the struggle with the same claims as workshop 2: 200 lire increase in base pay, promotion to the metalworker category. The management offered between 3 and 21 lire on the position allowance. The workers refused this offer. As long as we don't get everything we've asked for, the struggle will continue. On the lines the unions called a strike of 2 hours per shift. It was only partly successful. The line workers had been moving since Thursday against the work rates and for pay increases and category advancement, fighting independently of the unions.

The unions' request for the line delegate didn't mean these problems would be solved. The current struggle can't be reduced to the election of a delegate. On the engine and transmission assembly lines the workers strike for two hours per shift since Tuesday. They decided to fight for advancement to second category for everyone. Some of the preparation workers joined in. In the Presses the unions end the strike with laughable results. The workers were against it and production didn't return to normal. The workers don't want to return to the previous work rates and the bosses are worried. Fiat management is trying to get back to normal production at any cost because it has lost tens of millions in production precisely at the time when there's greatest demand in the market.

The unions try to start the struggles one at a time, one finishing and another starting, to avoid the struggle widening and to stop the workers organising themselves in the factories from expressing their will autonomously. But the working-class struggle won't be controlled this way. Almost every day a new struggle starts, and it's the workers who start it. This is a big test of the working class's strength. But it's not enough. There's a risk that while new struggles are started, others end with unsatisfactory results which will impede the formation of a strong and permanent organisation of workers who know how to oppose day by day the working conditions imposed by the bosses. If workers end up divided and disorganised after the struggle, this is a defeat, even if something has been gained. If workers come out of the struggle more united and organised, this is a victory, even if some demands remain unmet.

Friday 6 June: 8 hour strike each shift, not only in workshops 2 and 3 but also in the South Foundries. The struggle also continues in workshop 4. Saturday 7 June: Management suspends a worker from workshop 13 for three days. Monday 9 June: 8 hour strike in both shifts at workshop 13. The causes: no reason on the part of the management for the suspension of the worker and no response from the union to the workers' requests over: promotion to second category for all. Equal insurance for all. Workers' control over work rates. Equal bonuses for all. Increased downtime. Changes to the work environment. Wage increases that won't be absorbed into the national contracts.

North and South Foundries, 8 hour strike on both shifts. To divide the workers management offers a 67 lire increase to the press operators. Only 100 out of 890 accept. Body lines: First shift, spontaneous strike at 10 o'clock by the painting and polishing workers. Claims: wages, categories, work rates. The internal commission said it would reply by 8 o'clock, but was neither seen nor heard. Now they say they will reply next Monday. The supervisors came by on the second shift trying to divide the workers by giving second category to some of them. Fiat is cornered. Hardly any vehicles coming out, shortage of supplies for Rivalta and the organisation of work disrupted. This is the first result of our struggle. A decisive week starts now.

What does the boss do? In opposition to our struggle, the boss, with the complicity of the union, tries to make us participate in and consent to our exploitation. This is, in substance, what the line delegate is about. Against the workers' interests in widening the struggle at this point, they want to: either separate us from the rest of the Italian working class with a separate Fiat contract, like in '62, or fence us in with an advance on the future contract, which is the same thing. What does the union do? Attempts to halt the strikes in the individual workshops, comes into the factories to tell us what the boss proposes, takes its own proposals to the boss, negotiates them on our hides and ignores our will and our aims.

What do we workers want? At the Mirafiori North and South Foundries we've said it and said it again, with all-out strikes. We want: a 200 lire increase now on the base rate, or wage parity with the steelworkers. Which means 30,000 lire a month more on our base pay, and not the pittance the bosses have offered. On the assembly lines we want 50 lire more on the base rate. Second category for all workers after six months' work in the factory. We want this all right away. None of this is negotiable. None of this is an advance on the contracts. We don't want the boss's work rhythms. We say to the boss and the unions: The line delegate is no use to us. We want section meetings and workshop committees, which we'll use to organise a permanent struggle against the boss, his work rhythms, his servants. We'll organise ourselves, we'll all become delegates. Workers, when we fight the boss is weak, this is the moment to attack. We need to organise and widen our struggle, workshop by workshop.

Tuesday 10 June: The union's politics of dividing the workers by allowing category advancement to some and giving differentiated wage increases gets its first results. The struggle in the Foundries ends and the workers go back to work. The mechanical lines continue the strike for two hours. Some workers from the body workshop in workshop 54 are reorganising themselves and ask the comrades to intervene and prepare a leaflet listing their claims to distribute the next day. The workers from workshop 25, hot work, ovens, also request a leaflet for the next day.

Wednesday 11 June: The workers from the afternoon shift at workshop 54 have decided that if they don't get an answer to their claims by Friday they'll strike. The tendency to organise autonomously, renouncing union mediation for bargaining with the bosses, is spreading. In fact there are requests for leaflets from the workers of workshop 13, workshop 85, new sections of workshop 14 and the lines of the body workshops, and workers from the Foundries. As a result, Fiat's repressive politics gets worse. Two sackings at workshop 13 yesterday. Today the workers got six thousand lire less in their pay packets, deducted for time on strike.

Foundry workers: The boss is in crisis. Production, reduced by half, is further disrupted by initiatives of the workers who are fed up with waiting for the contract negotiations, which the boss is preparing to confront. If the struggle at the Foundries had lasted another few days, production in whole sections of Fiat would have stopped: Mechanics, Rivalta. But this time the boss had enough stock to allow production elsewhere at a reduced rate, and so was able to hold out longer than the workers. But anyway our struggle, leaving aside the limited results, has shown the boss our strength. We must use this strength to break the boss once and for all. It's a fact that here in the Foundries, where the struggle was harder and the workers, united, had resisted for longer, the boss resigned himself to conceding increases, even if they were differentiated and much lower than our claims. But this didn't happen on the lines, where the workers had also made wage claims.

But what raises did the boss concede? Our claims were: 200 lire more on the base wage or wage and conditions parity with the steelworkers, that is, 30,000 more a month in the pay packet. Because the work is hard and dangerous and we're not animals who work gratis. The union refused to put this claim, at the same time that it occurred to them to trumpet the management's offers. The increases offered by the bosses aren't on base pay but on the allowance for positions. This means that a transfer would lose you this advantage, and we know how easily the bosses can transfer you from one position to another. The 200 lire is the same for everyone because it unites the workers in the struggle and takes away the ability to discriminate that the boss uses against us.

Rather, the management offers that the union had outlined so well in their latest leaflet were divided by category, precisely to make the workers who would gain the most abandon the struggle one by one. So there is no point arguing among ourselves over it, because that is what the boss wants, to discourage our attempts at organisation. Because, comrades, this is the biggest victory in this struggle, apart from the boss's few miserable lire. For the first time we have succeeded in organising and conducting the struggle with our own aims, in the decisive moment for us. But that's not enough; the isolation of our struggle that the union wanted forced the Foundry workers to bear the full weight of the strike, when all the workers of Mirafiori wanted to fight.

Now we get it: the organisation we have created has allowed us to carry out the struggle in the factory, but it hasn't allowed us to overcome the isolation forced on us by the internal commission and the union. Refusing to carry our claims forward. Dividing the struggle of North Foundry from South Foundry. Not informing workers in Fiat's other sections. But the reasons we acted still hold. Just as we were able to organise ourselves in the workshop, we need to be able to organise all of Mirafiori. How? Only by cooperating with the workers of the other workshops will we be able to organise struggles that cause the least harm to us and the most harm to the boss. Only by making our full organised force felt will we force the boss to surrender.

Thursday 12 June: At Mirafiori the autolimitation of production by workers in workshop 13 continues. On the lines, on the 850, on the 124, on the 125, shortage of doors. At this point the management is too scared to carry out widespread reprisals. But they try to hit individual workers in the most advanced points of the struggle, sacking them or transferring them. They hope this will scare the rest. But this move mustn't go unchallenged. We need to respond blow by blow, stopping work as soon as a comrade is hit. The most effective weapon against this repression is unity and the workers' cooperation among themselves. The Fiat workers' struggle is spreading from Mirafiori to other firms. Grandi Motori, at Settimo, crane drivers and riggers. Grandi Motori Centro, sections P and B. Sima, lathe operators. Spa Centro, section 3.

All the Fiat Mirafiori workers who have been on strike in recent days have asked for the same thing: wage increases. Even the requests for category advancement mean: higher wages. And the same goes for increases in other components of the wage. But all of these claims had one common characteristic: the increases were claimed equally for everyone with automatic category advancement for everyone. Even the points on other matters tended to be the same for everyone. This means one fundamental thing: We want to get to an equal wage for everyone. In fact the workers have become aware that differences in wages, bonuses, categories, allowances and so on are one of the boss's tools for dividing workers.

In fact the boss, to avoid losing millions more in production, made use of the differential increases to bring an end to the struggle. He conceded category advancement to some workers but not others; for example, concession to leading hand on the lines, advancement for Maintenance. He conceded differential wage increases: for example, machine controllers and press operators in the Foundries. And in general on that part of the wage that encourages greater productivity or acceptance of danger: piece rates in the Presses, position allowances in the Foundries. The union delegates refused to be the spokesmen for the workers' claims for immediate equal wage increases for everyone.

They remain faithful to the principle that you request increases in the base wage only every three years when the contracts are up. They accept a series of divisive elements that the boss introduces regarding wages, categories, differentiation between various workshops and sections. Because of this they split the workers' general claims, dividing the struggle and creating confusion among the workers. But the workers want to get to an equal wage for everyone, because it eliminates divisions and unifies the struggle. Because then everybody inside the factory is indispensable, the technician as much as the worker, a machine or line specialist or a manual worker. Because now we can all do everything. Because living costs are the same for everyone.

So it doesn't make any sense for a clerk to be paid a full wage when he's off sick while a worker loses part of his wage. It doesn't make any sense for a clerk to get four weeks' leave and a 40-hour week, while a worker gets three weeks and works 44 hours. It doesn't make sense for some workers to be paid more and others less. Because of this, we Mirafiori workers won't be satisfied with delegates or increases of a few lire; we say: The struggle continues. And our struggle is joined by the workers at Spa Centro, with a march of 1,000 workers in the sections, at Grandi Motori, at Spa Stura, and also at Lingotto.

Monday 16 June: In workshop 54 at 5 o'clock the 124, 125, 125 Special lines are held up. Section heads, workshop heads and Fiat managers rush in and try to convince them to start work. Members of the internal commission also arrive and say that by Wednesday they'll have an answer. This time, however, the workers' reply is different and they say: While you talk, we're going on strike. After the evening meal break the 850 line also joins in, completely stopping production in workshop 84. The bosses ask why there's a strike and the workers reply: You know very well why. At this point the supervisors try to make the 850 workers finish 22 bodies that were still there, on the pretext that they would rust. The workers refuse, forcing the supervisors to get on the lines and finish the bodies.

It looks like the workers from workshops 1 and 3 of the Medium and Large Presses and also workshop 85, vehicle transport, will go again tomorrow. At 6 o'clock these workers, who drive the finished cars from the lines to the transporters, will have an answer from the union. If the union responds negatively to their claim over categories and being considered drivers rather than handlers, tomorrow they'll go on strike and push the vehicles instead of driving them. This could cause hold-ups in the line, because the yard would be flooded with vehicles within half an hour. The occupation of the Nichelino town hall also continues. In the past four weeks Fiat has lost tens of millions of lire in production and continues to lose more. Even in the last few days Mirafiori has produced only about fifty per cent of normal output in tons.

Tuesday 17 June: The struggle at Mirafiori is at its highest and most stirring point. In light of the ongoing strike on the second shift that is blocking all production on the lines, Fiat played a new card. The bosses now understand that the workers don't want anything to do with the unions. They have been forced to call directly on the striking workers to negotiate. After consultations with the unions, they ask the strikers to send delegates to the Unione Industriale.[22] Because they are used to wheeling and dealing, they delude themselves that they can con the workers with a few words. They offer them 17 lire, not for everyone, but on different components of the wage. But the workers won't let themselves be bought for small change.

And so the lord bosses, so well mannered and elegant, let loose with some foul insults. You terroni, filthy southerners, up until yesterday you were scratching in the dirt, and today you dare to raise your heads. The workers answered these insults right back in kind but what's more, once they were back in the factory, gave the kind of reply that counts for more, intensifying the struggle. A march of thousands of workers filled every corner of the factory, including the women's sections. To the cry of: Out, out, they stopped what little work was still going on. They stopped the 125 Special line and the 500 line again. Fiat is on its knees. In this uncomfortable position they play one last card. The twelve workers who had gone to the Unione Industriali were called up alone, without the unions, who are just about out of the game, to the office of Marciano, the deputy director of Mirafiori.

This guy invites them to convince their striking comrades to return to work because, let it be understood, very grave steps could be taken. If you haven't decided by this evening, he says, everything here will blow up, and if it goes on like this we will be forced to suspend people. If you suspend even one striking worker, the twelve reply, the whole factory will intensify the struggle. Fiat isn't prepared to negotiate on this basis, Marciano says, playing hard. And we're not prepared to work. And that is how, in fact, it goes. The second shift on the lines leaves the factory at eleven o'clock in the evening without having touched a single vehicle. At the gates it was so tense it seemed Torino was about to explode. Not a single union official was to be seen.

Wednesday 18 June: At six in the morning the workers on the first shift at workshop 54 returning to the factory learn what had happened the day before, about the great struggle their comrades in the second shift had continued and even widened. Yesterday the strike stuttered along, they say, today we'll hit like an avalanche. And that's how it goes. From one assembly line, the 124, only a single vehicle exits, from another, three or four cars. The 500 lines, after going along at a reduced rate themselves, stop completely. Both shifts are now on strike, all the lines stopped. At 1.30pm the workers from the first shift leave the factory with fists raised. And they are greeted with the same salute by the workers of the second shift who are re-entering the factory and who started the strike at Mirafiori.

The workers from the second shift continue the strike, solid. Fiat tries to make them work by running the lines empty. But after a short time it becomes clear even to the bosses that the workers are making fun of this move and the lines stop. A march starts from workshop 54 and disrupts workshops 52, 53, 55, 56. Not a single vehicle leaves the lines all afternoon. With the strike on the assembly lines completely under the workers' control, the march heads towards the management building. They meet the union delegates there, who try to deny everything that they have said against the strike in the past few days. They are no longer heard. The march moves towards the gates, where it blocks the truck exit. And finally it re-enters the lines, where a number of workers step up to speak to the meetings that are gathering all around.

Thursday 19 June: Comrade workers of Rivalta, yesterday in workshop 72 the workers suspended work for an hour. The request for uniforms was only a pretext, the reality is that the workers were protesting against exploitation and the brutish conditions inside and outside the factory. Inside because the bosses continue to up the work rates, making the work more and more unbearable. With work rates that make you spit blood without even time to eat or go to the can. Outside because the starvation wages are no longer enough to pay higher and higher rents and don't allow workers even the bare essentials of life. So workers are forced to live eight to a room or sleep on benches at the station. That's it, Fiat's workers are starved of money and want to work less.

Rivalta is at the most advanced point of technological development, the model of automation, the boss's jewel. All the special vehicle assembly lines have been transferred here. The 128 and the 130, the latest Fiat models, are built here. Today Fiat uses Rivalta to make up the increasingly bad losses caused by the struggle at Mirafiori, at least in part. They try to squeeze the workers, asking for production increases every day, pushing to the limit of the workers' resistance. The 128 line produces four extra vehicles a day. But workshop 72 signalled the beginning of the struggle. The bosses tried to pre-empt it, generously conceding some categories because they are scared that the struggle at Mirafiori will become the struggle at all of Fiat. And we know that all of Fiat in the struggle means beating the boss with objectives chosen and organised by the workers, workshop by workshop.

Friday 20 June: Comrade workers, for the fourth day the second shift in the body workshop has held up all production. The workers' marches have blocked every attempt to restart work. The first shift has also continued the struggle. On Wednesday only 30 vehicles came off out of more than 400 in normal production before the struggle. Production was drastically reduced yesterday as well. But this is not enough. The workers on the first shift must be as strong as their comrades on the second shift. Every variation in the consistency with which the struggle develops allows the bosses and their thugs to turn us against one another. To destroy every danger at its source there is only one response, unity in the struggle.

All output must be blocked. In the past month we have discovered that we have extraordinary strength. Only one workshop has to stop to hold up the whole factory. The organisation is growing and connecting up all the workshops, allowing the full use of this formidable weapon. This means that if the task of carrying the struggle forward today belongs to workshop 54, painting and polishing, other workshops must be ready to relieve them and must do so as soon as possible without waiting for the struggle in 54 to burn out. Today many workers intend to support the comrades of workshop 54, who are carrying the whole weight of the struggle, with donations. It's right but it is not enough. We must prepare ourselves to take our place in the struggle in all the workshops. We must meet with the workers of workshop 54 right away and coordinate the strikes. In this way the struggle will never be stopped again.

Today the union officials, who can't move freely outside the gates, have the boss's permission to hand out leaflets in the factory and spread false rumours. Here's what the union wants to say in the factory. Yesterday they told us that they had won 12 lire. But we have demanded: 50 lire on the base wage for everyone, advancement through the categories for everyone, breaks for everyone, without making up production.

Workshop 85 continues the struggle. Yesterday the Rivalta workers went into action and stopped the 128 line. Our action has been joined for two days by electronic control and data systems technicians. It is a powerful movement. That's what scares the radio and the newspapers, from La Stampa, which is silent or says little, to L'Unita, which spreads lies. To connect with each other, keep ourselves informed, discuss and direct the development of the struggle, meeting of all workers on Saturday 21 June at 4pm at Palazzo Nuovo in the University.

Saturday 21 June: At Mirafiori, as well as workshops 54, 85, 13 in the struggle, workshops 25 and 33 are also starting. Stop works at Rivalta. There have also been stoppages at Lingotto that point to a much wider struggle. At Spa Stura workshops 29 and 25 staged stop works for two hours all week. At Mirafiori workers from the other lines must substitute for those from 54 who were taking up the fight. Wherever claims have been made, there is no need to accept the bosses' constant stalling but to go right out on strike. In the Mechanical workshops many are saying it is not a good time to fight because Fiat has built up big stocks. But the strike would damage production at Rivalta and Lingotto.

Monday 23 June: Workers of 85, for a week we of 85 have been fighting in the way that we believe is best for us and most harmful to Agnelli with very precise claims: second category for everyone, the same as the comrades of 54. The lines have gone back to work for now but we will carry on with our claim for second category for everyone. As long as the lines are not held up they ignore our claims. Now they have extended the offer from six to seventy categories. They are trying to divide us in this as well by buying some of us off with promises. Let it be clear that we do not intend to negotiate our claim. Yesterday they even tried to make seconded hands work; they're nothing but scabs, and we responded accordingly. At South we ran them off. At North we completely stopped work, jamming up the lines from 9pm until 11pm. We should all remember: la lotta continua. It's either second category for everyone or we'll fill the piazzas.

Tuesday 24 June: Workshop 25 is completely at a standstill, all three shifts on strike for eight hours. Our warning to the managers: Pressuring us to unload the ovens is useless, reminding us of the value of the parts in the ovens is useless. It's your fault if you had them loaded because you knew the workers on the first shift intended to strike. But you didn't believe in our strength and so the strike has taken you by surprise. If you want to keep the Foundry working and want to avoid losses now you have to pay. The threatening letters you gave the workers on the first shift are a provocation that doesn't scare anyone. Workers of 25: now we have the upper hand. Our strike has direct consequences for all Fiat production. Yesterday after just eight hours of strikes the Mechanical workshop was already in trouble. Now they will start to run short of parts for Rivalta, Spa Stura and Autobianchi in Milano. We will continue the struggle.

Wednesday 25 June: Today at Mirafiori, preparations in 52 and 53 to stop all production, taking over from 54. Strike on both shifts. A march stops all production. We saw the team leaders get to work: the record belongs to team leader Bruno of 52, who made 13 bodies singlehandedly. Line 25 continues the strike solidly with 8 hours per shift. In section 42 of workshop 4, Foundry, 4 hours' strike. Autolimitation continues in workshop 16. Stop work in workshop 51. Stop works at Lingotto, at Materferro and at Carmagnola. The struggle has exploded at Rivalta. On the first shift, internal strike for two hours in workshop 64. Stop work in 72, 128 spray painting.

Stop work in 75 and 76, 128 line. On the second shift, internal strike from quarter to nine until knock-off in workshop 64, three teams. One hour stop work on two lines of the 128 modification and of half-an-hour for three turns of the 128 assembly in workshop 72. The situation has exploded and the bosses can no longer control it.

Thursday 26: Five weeks of strikes by only a few workshops at a time have cost Fiat more than 30,000 vehicles with a value of around 40 billion. Production has been more than halved. There's a shortage of parts for many models. Exports are held up. Because of this the management and the unions have reached a global agreement covering 60,000 workers. The agreement concedes differentiated increases, from 5 to 84 lire, on various components of the base wage. But how many will get 5 lire and how many 84 lire? The workers demand a 100 lire increase for everybody. The agreement maintains the distinction between categories, and in fact adds a new one, the super third. But the workers demand second category for everybody as the first step in doing away with categories. Differences in wages and categories are just a tool in management's hands for dividing workers. The struggle continues because the workers' demands have not been met.

Workshop 85: the strike continues for 8 hours. Workshops 52 and 53 body preparation: 8-hour strike with an internal march, first and second shift. All lines stopped due to shortage of parts. 700 assembled vehicles without engine blocks will have to be disassembled and put back on the line. Workshop 4, Foundries: 4-hour strike. Workshop 13: autolimitation of production continues. Workshop 26, Mechanical section: 2-hour stop work on the engine assembly line due to shortage of parts caused by the strike in workshop 25. Workshop 25: strike for 8 hours on three shifts with pickets around the finished units in case the management attempts to steal them. Lingotto: stop work for 15 minutes in workshop 10. The workers at Rivalta say no to the piss-weak agreement for 17 lire. On the first shift the workers blockade three lines: 124, 500, 850 for an hour, without the supervisors or the internal commission being able to stop them. On the second shift all of workshop 64 stops for 4 hours, the 128 line for just one hour. Stop work at Spa Stura, Grandi Motori, Carmagnola. Many supplying factories have now also stopped.

Friday 27 June: Workers of workshops 23, 24, 25, 26, 28, 41: Fiat has summarily dismissed 12 of our comrades from workshop 25 who were conducting an autonomous struggle for wage increases of 50 lire for everyone and for the second category. Fiat dismissed these workers to smash 25's struggle, which had paralysed the whole Mechanical section, and to demonstrate that it is dangerous to fight without the union. The workers of 25 reject this shameful blackmail and respond by continuing the struggle. They add the immediate withdrawal of these dismissals to the claims already presented, as a priority. Furthermore, the workers of 25 ask their comrades

154

in 23, 24, 26, 28, 41 to respond immediately to the provocative action of Fiat with stop works, meetings in the canteen, written requests to the management to withdraw the dismissals, marches to the gates of 25, collections to support the struggle and the dismissed comrades.

Saturday 28 June: Production halted at Mirafiori. At Rivalta many sections have stopped due to the strike in workshop 25 at Mirafiori and 64 at Rivalta itself. The strike at Carmagnola continues. At Lingotto the stop works occur with greater and greater intensity. The struggle spreads beyond Torino. To Fiat Modena. News arrives via flyers inserted in the engine packing cases by workers in Torino. To Fiat in Pisa. To Fiat in Naples. To Fiat in Florence. To Fiat in Trieste. To Piaggio at Pontedera. Everywhere in the same form and with the same aims. The Fiat strike also affects all the supplier firms. The conflict becomes tougher and tougher. The workers' organisation grows stronger and stronger. The bosses reply with a piss-weak agreement that is refused. They reply with dismissals, without the unions lifting a finger: two more dismissals at Aluminium, Carmagnola. They respond with intimidation: orders from the management to the heads to hand out warnings and suspensions to enable dismissals with just cause.

Agnelli resorts to gangsterism. Last evening a gang of hired thugs beat the shit out of comrade Emilio outside gate 5 at Rivalta where he was handing out leaflets. Five of them beat him savagely and rolled him into the middle of the street, trying to throw him under the passing cars. But discontent and the will to fight to the end against the bosses grows among all the workers of Torino. To try to recover this impetus to fight, the unions call a general action on Thursday 3 July to withhold rents. Saturday afternoon 28 June at 4.30 general assembly at Palazzo Nuovo, University, corner of Via Sant'Ottavio and Corso San Maurizio, beneath the Mole in Piazza Vittorio.

Ninth chapter **The assembly**

Comrades, what has emerged from the struggle at Fiat is above all workers' autonomy, workers resisting every type of union mediation. They have autonomously organised the form of the struggle, they have autonomously established its aims. And on this basis they have started to build an autonomous organisation that will allow them to take the struggle forward. Let's remember that this is the fifth week of the struggle at Fiat. What has emerged from this struggle above all is the workers' demand for unity, meaning: the claim for equal wage increases for all and the desire to overcome the divisions by category and position allowance that the boss and the union have introduced into the wage structure.

There has been a continual attempt by the unions to extinguish, to circumscribe and isolate this struggle which has primarily been articulated in negotiations at the level of the section and the workshop, until we arrived at the worthless agreement of a couple of days ago covering all of Fiat. This bullshit agreement has developed at the level of the enterprise the attempts that were made at the level of the workplace, which is to say: increases determined by the wage structure, which they maintain unaltered. Which is to say: nearly all of the increases in the variable part of the wage, position allowances and so on. What's more the workers' demand for second category for all has resulted in the introduction of the super third category by the union. A phoney category that is no more than the 17 lire increase camouflaged under the name of category and that increases the number of existing categories from 5 to 6.

Comrades, it seems clear that the working class of Fiat has refused the union's bullshit agreement everywhere. The struggle is carried forward, new struggles have been opened and those started before continue. Now we need a certain foresight in assessing what other means the boss might use to extinguish our struggle and above all to mystify its content. We can foresee some of these measures here, reprisals, the shutdown of Fiat, forced leave, bringing forward the negotiations and the contractual agreements and so on. And this assembly will also deal with evaluating the significance of this struggle, in regards to the national agreements. The day's last point of order will consider the general strike called by the unions for next Thursday. We can start the discussion immediately.

I would like to say, we have seen that with 45 days' struggle we have got 17 lire. We don't know what to do with it but we've got it. If we hadn't gone on strike for 45 days we wouldn't have managed even this. Going on like this we will be able to play a big role in the national agreements. Because the organisation that we are creating now will be important when strikes for the agreements are being considered. Then there's another thing I wanted to say. It's important to force their hand with the struggle in the coming days because Agnelli has been caught unprepared and hasn't had time to build up his stocks. In October any moron would know we were going to strike. Maybe a week, 15 days, 20 days. And Agnelli, who is not a moron, would know it too, and so would have built up his stocks.

If we pull the leash too tight, if he has threatened to stand us down now but hasn't, in October he'll close the gates and stand us down because he doesn't give a shit about us. This is the moment when the market demands the greatest production. It is the moment when Agnelli needs us the most and it is the moment to strike. Unite comrades, I don't know if there is anyone here from my workshop, I don't care about arselickers. But tonight I have plastered the toilets with leaflets. If anyone hasn't been to read them yet, go and read them now. The struggle at Fiat must become the Vietnam of the bosses in Italy. Applause.

Listen comrades. Yesterday they gave us letters, notices of suspension. This morning we heard about 12 dismissals, I have the letter in my pocket, I'll show you. In relation to the grave matters disclosed under your responsibility on the day of the 24th inst and already charged to you we hereby advise you of your dismissal, under article 38, section b of the standing national work agreement. You are requested therefore to make arrangement for the collection of your work documents and any remaining entitlements from our Administration office after 9 July 1969. Yours faithfully. Now all of us from workshop 25 agree that if we don't all return to work, including the twelve who were dismissed, here they are coming in now the others who have had the letter, then the strike will continue.

But there's one thing. Outside I met a union official, here at the university, and a few guys pulled me away, because I wanted to argue over what I told him: I want to meet, you and me. You're from the union, OK. We put forward our conditions, fifty lire. But, he said, when you went on strike all together, you didn't call me. But there was no need to call you because we can do things for ourselves. You've made a mistake, says he. But now, these twelve dismissals, what's to be done? Then he said he didn't know. I'll tell you what's to be done. You're from the union, so call all the workers at Fiat to go on strike and the rest all together. Because if there's another dismissal, what, will you get the strike going? Or how will it be done? He didn't answer.

Then I said, if at a certain point I take responsibility for the struggle, for my whole workshop, then all the other workshops have to join the strike with us. I went to 24 to ask them to be part of the strike. They said: No, because the PSIUP[23] is imposing it on us. This fucking PSIUP is giving me the shits. However you look at it, it's like this: if those of us who were

160

dismissed don't go into the factory, the workshop where I am, at least, won't go to work. Prolonged applause. Comrades, if signor Agnelli takes it on himself to dismiss ten, tomorrow he won't dismiss ten but five hundred. He'll dismiss a thousand, two thousand and kick us all out. But he is not the boss. We, the workers, are. While we in the factory earn a hundred thousand lire a month, signor Agnelli earns two hundred billion with our blood, it's us who spill blood. Let's strike inside and out, let's strike. Applause.

I would like to speak about Thursday's strike. We know that this strike has been called by the union in an attempt to take back control of our struggle. We have to try to exploit this strike over evictions or whatever it is in our own way, we mustn't let the union take the initiative. So it's about taking our strike, our struggle, outside and that's why we have to organise ourselves. In the three days that we have let's try to organise ourselves, team by team, section by section, workshop by workshop. And let's try to have a march big enough to get what we want, if not with words then with force. Applause.

Comrades, workers won't go into the streets to express their indignation if they are always controlled within the ambit of the party and the union. But they will go because they are fed up with the state of affairs and dare to speak their minds, dare to hit not just Agnelli but also the pseudo-revolutionary parties and their falsifying positions. Thunderous applause.

Comrades, some of you may have doubts about the risks, about the fact that there could be serious clashes at the march. But we say right away that the march is not a provocation but that it has the job of explaining the struggle in the factory to the city. To let it be known what has been going on in the workshops for more than a month and why. And that all the newspapers have done everything to avoid mentioning it. So with this we must let all Torino know that we won't stop for twenty or even thirty lire. We want what we have asked for and they must give it to us. Applause.

Voice from the floor: I want to propose to the workers who are planning to go on strike to include in the claims the re-hiring of the workers who were dismissed. First thing: we have to tell Agnelli that the struggle at Fiat won't be neutered with an increase of 17 lire. Second: that we won't be neutered even with the dismissal of the workers' vanguard. All workers must now know that the united response to these reprisals isn't a means of defending the comrade who has been defeated. It's a means to strike right at the bosses' power. It is a means of saying that we are fighting not so much for the dismissed worker as against the current system in the factory in Torino. We say openly that we will not allow dismissals. Repeated applause.

Comrades, I would just like to advise the comrades here that the struggle at Mirafiori continues, and on Tuesday at half-past five workshop 56 will go on strike with the same demands made by workshop 54 and the other workshops, 50 lire plus 50 lire and the categories. We will present our demands on Monday morning, giving them only 24 hours. Seeing as the testing workshop and workshop 19 are going on strike, we are aiming to go on strike on the same day. For anyone who doesn't know, if there is anyone from workshop 56 here, you are asked to get together with the others, because we are doing it. They think we're dickheads, because we've never been on strike, now we hope to be able to do something, too. That's all.

Comrades, it appears that from July 1 bread will cost twenty lire more and cigarettes 50. Newspapers have already gone up, the landlords want to raise rents and they are kicking us out. Everything has gone up, every product, even Fiat cars have gone up. And us, 17 lire an hour. But 17 lire is useless to us when everything is going up. We don't care a bit about the increase in the production bonus. I heard that right now we'll be paid at base rates because there's no production, because the daily quota of cars determined by the management isn't being produced. And I asked why. I was told: Because you work for piece rates. But who offered these piece rates to me? No one. I don't know anything about it, and just like me neither do the other workers. It was those well-known intermediaries between the workers and the management, the unions. We want what we have demanded, with force.

I was also told that now we should be satisfied with 17 lire if we want to conclude the agreement. The famous agreement that is supposed to be signed in October. Wastepaper, because we won't sign it. They've made it clear they want us to be calm, but that's not possible, we have needs, we need money. We have to have it, and no one can put a spoke in our wheels. They said that second category isn't possible after six months of employment, because it would send the boss broke. But that is exactly what we want, who cares if the boss goes broke, him and his shitty factory. Applause.

Comrades, the situation in Torino and surrounds is a setback for the bosses. Fiat lets us live, Fiat kills on the lines. Outside the factory, you want lodgings, then you work at Fiat, room and board makes 30,000 lire a month plus expenses for electricity etc. Exploited inside the factory and out. I work in workshop 25, which seems like a prison, actually a cell, where you find every type of lowlife. Production at Fiat: ten workers absent and in the end you still make the quota. Who suffers? We do. Transport more and more expensive. Who suffers? We do. No one cares and we suffer, we are democratically slaves of the boss.

Let's fight, with the good, with the bad, but let's fight all out. We have negotiated from 10 per cent to around 12 per cent. How was it done? We have to fight, fight, fight for more money and less work. We need to abolish capitalism and be treated like men, not beasts of burden. Capitalism is a rotten and broken system. No one can stand it any more. The young reject it, even the young bourgeois students who we see here among us. And all the workers know on how much suffering and how much injustice it has fattened itself. Keep at it, stick to the struggle, comrades, don't be fooled by the bosses, don't let yourselves be fooled by the union. Applause.

Comrades, earlier I heard about comrade Emilio, who got a beating. I heard the day before from a fascist who works with my wife that signor Agnelli offered thousands for the fascists to provoke any of the groups gathered near the gates. I thought it was just talk, but knowing that they gave Emilio a beating, I think this is happening. We know they gave Emilio a beating and they'll give others beatings. But the best thing is this, that Agnelli has finished using his tactics, his so-called modern and democratic tactics. In the past he had the unions as his lackeys but now they've bombed completely. They're not there now, they don't know what to do, they're no use to him any more.

Now he's trying to get tough, which is capital's last resort. I mean, when you take a hit, at first you try to play fair. Then when he sees that he can't take it he rounds up the various action squads.[24] Well, he'll get it too. What happens, happens. We reply to Agnelli that it is not so much our struggles that strengthen our will, but he himself who has shown us that he's on the ropes. So I say this, whatever he does now he can't break the workers' will. He can't kid himself, he already knows it very well. Workers are developing another mindset, they understand what they have to do. Maybe only a few, maybe a vanguard, but that is the important thing. I don't speak from others' experience. In four years I have changed completely, before I had what you might call a petit bourgeois mindset, I believed that by being good you would get everything.

Today I am, let's say, a revolutionary. They call us that, or cinesi,[25] they don't even know themselves. Anyway, I wanted to say, there will be provocations at the march, but we will march all the same. I say no one can stop us now. And there's another thing: we don't criticise the Communist Party just for the sake of criticising it. It's logical that the revolution won't happen tomorrow or the day after, but I do say this: the worker's mindset is too advanced now and the Party is trying to hold it back. It's logical that we need to take one step at a time, but ultimately, when there's the base, when there's the mass pushing from below, that says everything is a mess, in a disruptive manner, the Party keeps holding back, and the union too.

And they keep saying: an apolitical union, as a comrade pointed out earlier. But I reply. Are you taking the piss? Do you really think we're still morons who believe that the union can possibly be apolitical? But that's how completely fucked they are now. They're mercenaries, and they'll be treated like mercenaries. So carry on like that, you unionists. Take the bosses' money, your time will come. Then see, we'll make you a nice casket. Applause. Agnelli is on the ropes, capitalism in its phase of development is on the ropes, all our enemies are on the ropes. So we'll continue the struggle and we will never stop, never. Let Agnelli and all his worms be warned. Long applause.

Comrades, as you all know every day the percentage of absences at Fiat is extremely high. It's people who can't take the murderous work rates imposed by the bosses any more. It's people staying at home to preserve their own physical existence. It's a constant flight from productive work. It's about the right to be healthy, of struggles against harm. But that's not to say that the only question is that work is harmful. The immigration of young people from the south to Fiat has gone on at an increasing rate in recent months. The constant resignations by workers who no longer want to suffer at Fiat, and the sackings of workers who are absent too often is a given. All of this suits Fiat because the new workers get a lower wage for the first four years of exploitation in the factory.

Add to this the vicious circle that takes almost your whole wage away. The young immigrants who go back and forth between the trattoria and the rooming house. Six or seven years ago you could save money to repay your debts from moving north and send money orders home to the south. The real wage at Fiat has gone backwards in the past few years. This is the reason for our strike for Battipaglia, why Battipaglia was the end of the meridionalist politics of the DC and the PCI in the south, of the state and the monopolies, the chance for a political strike against Fiat and the state's planning.

As far as Thursday's strike goes, it wasn't the unions who realised that the workers couldn't cope with the rents any more. It was the workers with their acts of rebellion, outside every union and political line, who showed they'd had it up to here with increases in the cost of living and in rents. And that at a certain point they can no longer be satisfied with the starvation wages that you get today. We demand a guaranteed wage, we demand to be paid according to our needs, whether we are working or whether we are unemployed. Applause.

Comrades, now after all these weeks of strikes in which we have brought the bosses to their knees, everyone tells us not to overdo it. The unionists tell us in the factories, the newspapers tell us outside. That if things go on like this there will be a crisis, that we must be careful because all of this lost production is destroying the Italian economy. And then we'll all be worse off, there will be unemployment and hunger. But it doesn't really seem like that to me. Let's leave aside the fact that, as the previous comrade said, if the bosses' economy crashes we don't give a shit. In fact, we'd love it.

Nothing is truer, but there's another thing. And that is that we don't give a shit because we know that as long as nothing changes it's us who are worse off. Isn't it us who always pay the highest price in every struggle? Comrades, I'm from Salerno, and I have done every kind of work in the south as well as the north and I have learned one thing. That a worker has only two choices: a gruelling job when things are going well or unemployment and hunger when they go badly. I don't know which of the two is worse. But anyway, it's not as if a worker can decide for himself, it's always the boss who decides for him.

When we're pissed off because we just can't take it anymore it's useless coming and begging us to go back to work. Moralising about how we're all one country, with common interests, that everyone has his role to play and his duty and all of that. That the stomach cannot eat if the arm no longer works and so the whole body dies. So they threaten us and beg us to go back to work because if we don't it will be worse for us too. But it's not like that, because as I said earlier from our point of view as long as they have the power, they're killing us either way, whether we work or not.

So we won't fall for that any more, because we really aren't one body, us and them. We have nothing in common, we're worlds apart, we're enemies and that's it, us and them. Our biggest strength is being finally convinced that we have absolutely nothing in common with the work of the bosses and the

State of the bosses. In fact, our interests are the opposite. All of our material objectives are against this economy, they're against this development, they're against the general interest, which is that of the bosses' State. Now they tell us that Fiat is building a factory in Russia, in Togliattigrad, and that we should go there to learn how to work the way you work under communism.

But what the fuck do we care if workers in Russia are exploited too, if they are exploited by the socialist state instead of the capitalist boss. It means that is not the type of communism that works. And in fact it seems to me that they think more about production and about going to the moon than the people's wellbeing. Because wellbeing comes before everything else in allowing us to work less. And that is why now we say no to the terrified bosses when they ask us to help them with their production, when they explain to us that we have to take part, that it is in all our interests, too.

We say no to the reforms that the unions and the party want us to fight for. Because we understand that those reforms only improve the system that the bosses exploit us with. Why should we care about being exploited more, with a few more apartments, a few more medicines and a few more kids at school. All of this only advances the State, advances the general interest, advances development. But our aims are against development, they're against the general interest, they're ours and that's it. Our aims, the interests of the working class, are the mortal enemy of capital and its interests.

We started this great struggle by demanding more money and less work. Now we know that this is a call that turns everything upside-down, that sends all the bosses' projects, capital's entire plan, up in smoke. And now we must move from the struggle for wages to the struggle for power. Comrades, let us refuse work. We want all the power, we want all the wealth. It will be a long struggle, years, with successes and setbacks, with defeats and advances. But this is the struggle that we have to start now, a violent fight to the end. We must fight to end work. We must fight for the violent destruction of capital. We must fight against a State founded on work. We say: yes to working-class violence.

Because it's us, the proletariat of the south, us mass workers, an enormous mass of workers, the one-hundred-and-fifty-thousand workers of Fiat who have developed capital and its State. It is us who created all the wealth that exists, of which they leave us only the crumbs. We created all this wealth by dying of work at Fiat or dying of hunger in the south. And it is us, the great majority of the proletariat, who don't want to work and die any more for the development of capital and its State. We can't keep this crap going any more.

So now we say it's time to end it, because they don't know what to do with all this enormous wealth that we produce in the world other than waste it and destroy it. They waste it making thousands of atomic bombs or going to the moon. They destroy fruit, peaches and pears by the ton, because there's too much and it isn't worth anything. Because for them everything must have a price, it's the only thing they care about, products without value can't exist as far as they're concerned. It can't just be for people who don't have food, according to them. But with all the wealth that exists people don't need to die of hunger any more, they don't have to work any more. So we'll take the wealth, we'll take everything.

Are we all going mad? The bosses who make us work like dogs destroy the wealth we've produced. But it's time to be done with these people. It's time for us to fuck these pigs off once and for all, to get rid of them all and free ourselves for ever. Listen, State and bosses, it's war, it's a struggle to the end. Forward, comrades, forward like at Battipaglia, let's burn everything here, let's sweep this lowlife away, let's sweep this republic away. Very long applause.

Tuesday 1 July. Comrade workers of Rivalta, after the internal stop works of the past week, yesterday many workers went back to work. This doesn't mean that everything is finished and that we return to normal. The basic reason for this pause in the struggle is the general strike called by the unions for

Thursday. In fact many workers stopped their struggle yesterday and postponed everything until Thursday. This is dangerous, because the workers are organising themselves in the factories, where they are strongest, whereas Thursday's strike is about breaking this organisation and bringing everything to an end in a single day. But the unions are fooling themselves if they think everything will end, because the workers know how to use this opportunity to strengthen their struggle and their aims. The strike will happen as part of the great struggle the workers of Fiat have carried on for 45 days now.

The strike won't be to end the struggle and accept the crappy agreement that the unions want at any price, but must be used by the workers to strengthen the struggle for their aims, which haven't changed. The unions have called Thursday's strike about the problem of housing. But the problem of rents can't be separated from the struggle in the factories. It is with these struggles, and not by whining to the prefect, that a real working-class force will be built. Comrade workers, on Thursday morning we meet outside the factory to discuss how to carry on the struggle in the days to come. In the afternoon a march by all Fiat workers leaves from Mirafiori gate 2 in Corso Tazzoli at 3pm.

Wednesday 2 July. Today the struggle continues with stop works at Rivalta and in workshop 13 at Lingotto and is about to start again on the lines. The unions are threatening not to sign the agreement, the phony agreement that the workers have already refused by continuing the struggle, if the dismissals of the previous week are not revoked. To offer the unions, who are already completely discredited, a chance to get back in the game, the management revoked the dismissals straight away. Without a single hour of strike being called, something that had never happened in the previous twenty years.

The attempt at intimidation was completed by the sudden appearance of police and Carabinieri at the gates of Mirafiori. As if the sight of them could stop our struggle. Nor will we let ourselves be intimidated by the police during the march tomorrow. If the bosses think they can use the police to stop our struggle, try sending them into the factory to make us work in the workshops when we're deciding to strike.

Tenth chapter **The insurrection**

The evening before we'd gone to paste up posters all over the city, in every quarter. It was a poster of a clenched fist. On it were the aims of our day of struggle and the time: three o'clock at Mirafiori gate 2. At five in the morning we went to Mirafiori with megaphones. There were already loads of police outside even at five in the morning. Two or three hundred at least counting the jeeps, vans, prison vans and police and Carabinieri trucks. There were two at every gate and at least fifty outside the office building. We went to each gate at five in the morning using megaphones to explain to the workers of the first shift that they shouldn't go in, but no worker did.

There wasn't even any need to picket. Evidently the police were waiting for us to picket, so they could provoke us and attack us. On and off they hassled us, saying we shouldn't be using the megaphone and we shouldn't be in front of the gates. We said: We're using the megaphones because there's a strike, it's not like we're standing there with pistols threatening people to stop them going in. If they want to go in, fine, they go in, if they don't want to, then they don't go in. It's just a political action. There were no more than three or four scabs who tried to go in, and the police jumped in to block anyone who tried to stop them. But the night shift workers coming out of gate 1 pushed them back out.

No one went in, no one at all. They had all come, the workers, but they all stayed on the other side of the street. To check whether anyone went in. But no one was going in, and after a while everyone went home. In the afternoon we went to the gates with the megaphones for the second shift. We were supposed to meet at three o'clock outside gate 2. We got there a few at a time and there were already lots of workers waiting. Apart from the workers from the second shift who hadn't gone in, there were also loads of workers from the first shift who'd gone back to Mirafiori for this march.

By three o'clock there were already three thousand workers outside Mirafiori. Police were guarding all the streets that lead to Mirafiori, as well as all the gates, the office buildings and all that. Reinforcements had been coming since morning. There were no incidents at the union demonstration in the morning. They'd held their rally over housing with workers from the small and medium-sized factories, where they were strong, while at Fiat they barely existed. Outside gate 2 there were lots of red flags, signs and banners. While we were there waiting for the march to begin the police started up their provocations.

But what the police hadn't thought about, what the commissioner hadn't thought about, what the interior minister hadn't thought about, what Agnelli hadn't thought about, was that you weren't dealing with the usual student march, the so-called march of extremists. Or as the bourgeois newspapers said, the usual rich kids who have fun playing at revolution.

The workers who met outside Mirafiori gate 2 were the same workers who had been fighting at Fiat for all those weeks. They were workers who had been in hard struggles, victorious struggles. While the start of the march was being organised, the police began their manoeuvres. To one side they set a double cordon of Carabinieri who linked arms and pushed the demonstrators back. Other platoons of Carabinieri lined up in fours and advanced slowly into the middle of the demonstrators.

While deputy commissioner Voria gave these orders, moving the Carabinieri to surround us, he told a worker to move away from him. But this worker threw a punch that laid him out flat on the ground. Meanwhile the platoons of Carabinieri who were manoeuvring came on at a trot, jogging like Bersaglieri,[26] right into the middle of the demonstrators. And they were holding their rifles like cudgels, like clubs. Suddenly the charge sounded, which naturally no one fucking heard.

Then the teargas started to land, a dense mist of teargas, and everyone instinctively ran. Everyone ran and the Carabinieri began cracking us all with their rifle butts. They pushed us against the cordon of Carabinieri who held fast to surround us. I was right next to the cordon, their faces were pale, white, green with terror. Because they found themselves so close to us, face to face. A little while before I'd wound one up, I told him: Just wait, I'll take your pistol and shoot you with it. He didn't say a word.

They grabbed a comrade and wanted to drag him off, but they couldn't because we pulled him away and threatened them. Meanwhile with the sudden mist of teargas they dispersed the crowd around Mirafiori. We all ran away from the front of Mirafiori, and then the Carabinieri who had formed the cordon took their rifles, which they'd had on their shoulder straps, in their hands like clubs and came after us. It was a nice little massacre, they belted us madly with their rifle butts. Then they arrested about ten comrades. Just because we were there, without sticks, without stones. While I'm running I come upon a load of Carabinieri, ten of them, beating the shit out of a comrade who was stretched out on the ground. I yelled at one of them: What the fuck, do you want to kill him?

The guy gives me a dirty look, then he turns and takes off with the others, dragging this comrade along behind them. Then while I was there, about three or four metres away I saw a comrade, a student who was running with four or five Carabinieri after him. One catches him, and he smashes him in the head with his rifle, cracks his skull. I run over with some other guys and the Carabinieri take off. We get this comrade who's on the ground out cold and carry him away. We leave him with some women who were standing in a doorway. Because by now everyone from the surrounding buildings had come down into the street or out on their balconies, women, kids and babies, to see what was going on.

They had more or less managed to disperse us, but they hadn't reckoned with the workers' will to fight. Ten thousand people gathered between Corso Agnelli and Corso Unione Sovietica. There were tram tracks there with cobblestones between them. They start to fly at the police and the Carabinieri. And so they started to take a few hits, too. We got the march going that they had stopped at first. A policeman had been disarmed, his shield and helmet were taken off him and raised like trophies. There were banners that said: Potere operaio, and: La lotta continua. Suddenly a police ambulance sped into the middle of the march. It charged into the middle of the march with its siren wailing for no reason. Then it turned back the other way slowly. It was another provocation by the police. But the march starts and turns towards Corso Traiano.

Corso Traiano is right in front of the Fiat office building. Corso Traiano has two roadways and a lane in the middle with tram tracks and cobblestones. We came marching down on the right and the police advanced from the opposite direction. They stop and wait, blocking the traffic. They wanted to cut off our path, they didn't want to let us move from there. That is, they wanted to restrict the struggle to Fiat, around Fiat, not let it spread into the city. They thought that we wanted to head into the city centre, and in fact that was our idea.

People watched us from the windows along Corso Traiano as the march advanced. They appeared on the balconies, came down and listened to what we had to say. They were all with us because it was all workers who lived around there. Then suddenly teargas grenades come from the police line in front of us. An insane amount, unbelievable this time, firing them at people so they ended up everywhere. They were landing on the first-floor balconies, with the gas spreading through the apartments because it was summer and all the windows were open. More grenades landed on parked cars, smashing them and setting fire to them. And this really pissed off the people who lived around there.

Meanwhile a truck loaded with Fiat 500s entered Corso Traiano, a big transporter. We threw stones at the cabin and the driver got out. We started to smash up the cars with stones, then we put a rag in the tank. We lit it to blow up the truck, but the diesel didn't ignite. So we started to push it in neutral towards the Corso and we left it there across the street. They called the fire brigade, and when the fire brigade arrived they copped stones, too. We didn't let them move the truck, so the truck stayed where it was.

180

It was four o'clock, and that was the start of a battle that would last for more than twelve hours. The police circled and charged, and from the other side the Carabinieri moved in to close us in. We didn't disperse and right away we responded with stones that we collected from all over. Most of us moved into the park beside Corso Traiano, where there was also a building site. We armed ourselves with timber, sticks, material for building barricades. And there was a big pile of stones.

We got into this park, and the police came with their wagons and the Carabinieri with their trucks. The Carabinieri copped a barrage of stones, because they were out in the open and it was easy to hit them. We came right up to the trucks to attack them with sticks, and they threatened to fire on us with their machine-guns, and we stopped. So they took off. The police in armoured vans heard this constant din, the heavy rain of stones falling on their vans, and there's no way they wanted to get out. We'd surrounded all the vehicles, hurling stones from all sides. As soon as they got out we would have beaten the shit out of them with the sticks. We even tried to overturn a couple of the vans. The guys inside, terrified, told the drivers to get out of there, and in fact they took off, the lot of them.

A quarter of an hour later they tried again, coming into the park on foot. With shields, helmets, batons, rifles with teargas grenades. We were waiting for them in the park. They came to within fifteen or twenty metres of us. We started to taunt them, saying: Why don't you try to get us now, like you did outside gate 2? We'll fuck you up good. Only one of them answered: Come out on your own, we'll go man to man, I'll fuck you right up I will and so on. But they didn't move, they were scared.

We had all these stones, and more stones and sticks and clubs on the ground in front of us. They waited there for a bit, then they gave the order to fire the teargas and charge. But they hadn't thought about being in the park, in an open space. So you could see the teargas grenades as they landed, and we grabbed them and threw them back so that they were surrounded by the smoke as much as we were. We threw stones, and as they weren't protected when they were running they copped heaps. When they realised they couldn't do anything, they took off like rabbits and we went after them with sticks.

Meanwhile the people of Corso Traiano had had a gutful of the teargas landing on the balconies and in the windows and the smoke spreading through their apartments. The police beat anyone they found in the doorways. Women, old people, children, whoever they found. They especially beat the kids, even ten- and eleven-year-olds. Everyone had joined in to fight with the workers. Youths throwing stones, the women handing out wet handkerchiefs to counter the gas. Comrades being chased by the police found refuge in apartments. Everyone was throwing things at the police from the windows and the balconies.

The police came after us from all over, scattering us and dividing us into lots of small groups. Even in the side streets you couldn't breathe because of the smoke. I'm with some students who decide to go to the Faculty of Architecture, which is occupied, for a meeting and to get back together with the other groups. As we are heading out of there a column of armoured vans with sirens appears. We split into two groups, one that heads to Architecture and one that stays to fight.

While people were arriving at the Architecture faculty, and the red flag had been run up the flagpole, the Carabinieri come. They charge, fire teargas, arrest about a dozen comrades. We defend ourselves, we fight back with stones. So they don't get into the university. They fire teargas through the windows, but a group of us fight back with stones and stop them getting in while we hold a meeting. More comrades arrive and tell us that the clashes in Corso Traiano have spread and are getting bigger and that there were big clashes at Nichelino.

The news is that at Borgo San Pietro, at Moncalieri and in other communes around southern Torino there have been clashes. There's fighting in all the working class neighbourhoods. Meanwhile, outside the university the charges and the stone throwing were getting more violent. The fighting was spreading along the main street, into the side streets, into the entranceways. Teargas, rocks, hand-to-hand, solid. It's decided to divide into squads and head to the various quarters of the city

that were fighting. To check how far the clashes had spread.
I'm with a squad of comrades going to Nichelino. To get to
Nichelino we had to go along Corso Traiano.

We get back to Corso Traiano around half-past six and we
see an unbelievable battlefield. It happened that the building
workers and the other workers who lived in the neighbourhood were going home. They hadn't been part of the strike,
they knew fuck all about it. They were coming back home and
saw all this smoke, all these police, the street full of rocks and
rubbish. So they joined the comrades right away and started
to pile building supplies into the street to make barricades.
Because there were lots of building sites around there, so there
were bricks, timber, wheelbarrows, those metal drums full of
water, cement-mixers.

They put it all in the middle of the road, and made barricades
with cars, and then set it all alight. The police hung back at the
end of Corso Traiano, towards Corso Agnelli. Every so often
they took off on a sortie, a charge. They cleared the barricades
while people pelted them with stones and then ran into the
park at the side. Then they went back when the police had left.
They carried the stuff back into the street and rebuilt the barricades with planks of wood and whatever. They poured petrol
on it all and when the police advanced again they set fire to
it. And they set fire to tyres and rolled them, flaming, at the
police. Molotov cocktails started to appear.

There were red flags on some of the barricades; on one there was a sign that said: *Che cosa vogliamo: tutto*. People kept coming from all around. You could hear a hollow noise, continuous, the drumbeat of stones rhythmically striking the electricity pylons. They made this sound, hollow, striking, continuous. The police couldn't surround and search the whole area, full of building sites, workshops, public housing, fields. People kept attacking, the whole population was fighting. Groups reorganised themselves, attacked at one point, scattered, came back to attack somewhere else. But now the thing that moved them more than rage was joy. The joy of finally being strong. Of discovering that your needs, your struggle, were everyone's needs, everyone's struggle.

They were feeling their strength, feeling that there was a popular explosion all over the city. They were really feeling this unity, this force. So every rock that was hurled at the police was hurled with joy, not rage. Because in a word we were all strong. And we felt that this was the only way to defeat our enemy, striking him directly with sticks and stones. The neon signs and the billboards were battered. The traffic lights and all the poles were smashed and pulled down. Barricades went up everywhere, with all kinds of things. An overturned steamroller, burnt electricity generators. When darkness fell you saw fires everywhere among the teargas fumes, molotov cocktails flying, flames.

I couldn't get into the middle of the fighting with the police. Loads of comrades had got there before me, coming from all over. You couldn't see for smoke and there was noise and confusion. The police were quickly pushed back towards the end of Corso Traiano with lots of us chasing them. We faced off with the police and fought at the edge of the park. There was one policeman on the ground, who moved now and again. A load of our guys chased the police across the tram tracks and a huge cloud of black smoke rose from the burning cars. Our guys swirled all around, you saw them go into the smoke and come out and you heard lots of explosions.

Everything was confused, people yelling and running back and forth. When we got near the end of the street it looked like the clashes had already been going on for a while. We came across a comrade bleeding from his mouth and we hoisted him onto our shoulders. Further on we came across another comrade who was bleeding and couldn't stay on his feet. He kept getting up and falling over again. When we got right near the end we could see the police. They had got out of the vans and were standing in a group with their helmets and their shields.

They were waiting for us and firing teargas. We had just about surrounded them, from every side. I could hear some of our guys shouting: Get out of here. And I saw that lots of policemen were scared and were running away. All around our guys started to chant: Ho Chi Min. Forward, forward. They rushed forward and the air grew dark with dust and smoke. I saw bodies moving around me like shadows and the noise of explosions, sirens and shouting was really loud. At one point I saw a policeman right in front of me and I got into him with a stick. The policeman fell under foot as everyone ran.

At the end we turned back down the road and there were loads of injured people there, too. We'd cleared the police right away. We were all crazy with happiness. We waited there a bit longer and after a while we saw a line of trucks coming from one of the cross streets. Everyone began to shout: forward, forward. And we took off chasing the police who were running back the way they'd come. One was hit and we went after him, still hitting him. Then we chased the police back to the end of the cross street they'd come out of.

Meanwhile they keep firing teargas everywhere, the air more and more unbreathable, and we have to retreat. The police gradually retake Corso Traiano, but barricades are continually thrown up one behind the other. People who are caught get the shit beaten out of them and get thrown into the prison vans. Lots of police get beaten up. At the same time police reinforcements arrive. They come from Alessandria, from Asti, from Genova. The battalion from Padova that came in the morning wasn't enough. But the clashes keep spreading.

The fighting becomes fiercer outside the Fiat office building, in Corso Traiano, in Corso Agnelli, in all the side streets. In Piazza Bengasi, where the police charge like animals, absurd, senseless violence. But they are attacked from two sides and only escape being surrounded by the skin of their teeth. Deputy commissioner Voria is almost captured. Comrades listening to police radio say they have requested authorisation to open fire.

The comrades block the attacks with more barricades in the smoke and flames. Small groups attack the police, throwing molotovs then escaping into the park in the darkness. Still the low drumming sounds on the pylons. Car bodies in flames. The streets all stripped of paving stones and a huge number of rocks scattered all over the place. The police's behaviour gets worse and worse, they're like animals. Teargas is fired at people and directly into apartment buildings to stop people coming out and showing themselves. Deputy commissioner Voria is seen brandishing a grenade launcher and warning people to get out of the windows. Then with more reinforcements arriving the police start to take control of the zone. Later they enter apartment buildings, going right into people's apartments, where people live, to arrest people, making hundreds of arrests. Even an old woman who gives the police a bit of lip is arrested.

In Piazza Bengasi the attacks and rock barrages continue. The police reinforcements have arrived, and they no longer have to restrict themselves to controlling Mirafiori like before, every now and again making charges to relieve the pressure. Now they're able to control the whole area. They surround Piazza Bengasi, go into the entranceways of the apartment buildings, rounding people up even in their apartments. At midnight there are still clashes going on. All around Corso Traiano you hear them shouting at the police who drag people out of their apartments: Bastards, pigs, Nazis. They shout from the windows: This is like the Nazi round-ups, you bastards.

So then we decide to go to Nichelino where the battle has been going on all afternoon. It wasn't easy to get to Nicheli-no, in the sense that you couldn't get there by the usual way, which was blocked by a barricade of burnt-out cars. The bridge into the neighbourhood was blocked too. We come by another minor street that leads right into the neighbourhood. All those immigrants, the thousands of proletarians who lived at Nichelino, had built barricades all over the place with cement pipes. They'd pulled down the traffic lights and thrown them into the street. Loads of stuff from building sites was piled in the middle of the street to make barricades, which were then set alight.

Via Sestriere, which crosses Nichelino, is blocked by a dozen barricades of burning cars and trailers, road signs, rocks, timber. In the night huge bonfires of tyres and wood are burning. An enormous fire burns with timber from an apartment block under construction. The whole building site is in flames. The street lights have been smashed with stones and in the dark all you see are flames. The police tried to stall, they left us alone, they held off. They attacked around four in the morning, when reinforcements came. Almost all the workers were exhausted, they'd been fighting for more than twelve hours, while they, the police, had reinforcements.

They'd been waiting there at the barricades, waiting for morning, when fresh troops would arrive to relieve them. We had turned back to defend the bridge blocked by burning cars with rocks, where the reinforcements wanted to pass. But there weren't many of us left defending the bridge, only twenty or so. Then the jeeps and the trucks with reinforcements came through the side street where we had come in, and to avoid being surrounded we all had to run. Some Carabinieri got out of a truck and came after us firing teargas.

We all fled, chased by the Carabinieri. At one point we saw a line of jeeps coming towards us, right in front. I don't know how they ended up there, maybe they were coming back from a patrol. Things were turning bad for us. So we all ran at the police, yelling and throwing stones at the jeeps to chase them off. Then we saw that the Carabinieri were behind us, and so we turned around and attacked them. But loads of police were coming up behind the Carabinieri. So we had to run because there were only a few of us left.

By now I was exhausted and I ran like crazy. I got to a field, stumbled on a rock and nearly lost my shoe. When I stopped to look for my shoe a Carabiniere appeared who'd been chasing me on his own. Then I saw a comrade who was running with me jump the Carabiniere. They fought hand to hand and the Carabiniere went down. At one point I saw smoke at the top of a street. We got to the top of the street and from there you could see a wide avenue where the fighting continued. You couldn't tell who was winning. Everything was so confused. I just wanted to stop somewhere for a shit, I couldn't hold on any more.

Some Carabinieri attacked us and I couldn't get into the middle where the fighting was hardest. Right then we heard someone shouting: They're coming, they're coming. I saw a huge cloud of smoke rising in the middle of the road and everyone ran back and forth yelling. Then out of the smoke the police appeared in armoured vans with spotlights illuminating everything. They looked big and strong and they were all firing teargas. There was a building site beside the road and a group of us were gathering there. The comrade who was with me headed for the building site and I followed him.

A whole lot of people were running off together down the street. I looked back and saw them all running and scattering into the side streets. When we got to the building site there were already quite a few others there. The police were firing teargas over our heads and knocking down pieces of wood and bricks. We couldn't see what was going on in the street any more. It was all smoke and shouts and blasts. The street was obscured by smoke and dust and there were only shadows and a din of shouting and sirens and explosions. To my left I heard the roar of motors and the sirens of the police vans that were going back up the street. Two molotovs burst in the middle of the street.

There was smoke and teargas everywhere, you couldn't breathe. Then the police got out of the vans and ran towards us. They ran through the smoke with masks and shields. I found myself among a lot of our guys who were running back and forth and scattering into the side streets. The police ran after us and we were all there mixed up in the gloom lit by fires and a huge racket. I couldn't see much, but once I saw one of our guys lay into a policeman who'd been left behind and hit him again and again with a stick.

I saw some police come running out of a side street on our left. We all raised our sticks and threw ourselves at them in the half-light surrounding us. I ran into a policeman with a helmet and hit him. He cried out and fell headlong to the ground.

Then we all went back towards the road. On the other side of the road we saw a group of our guys hurling themselves at police who were going back towards the vans. The police fled and we all went after them, chasing them back to the end of the street where the vans were waiting with engines running and spotlights illuminating the road. There was a policeman with his arms raised, groaning. I saw a few of our guys helping a kid get up. I saw that he was injured and bleeding from his head.

With the help of more reinforcements the police slowly took back ground. They started rounding up people house by house, pitiless, brutal. But people didn't run. Workers and locals relieved each other, they were all used to the teargas by now and they kept on building barricades. Four or five of us being chased by about twenty Carabinieri get to the door of an apartment building and we close it behind us. I climb over a little bit of wall in the courtyard and find myself in a workshop. In the workshop there was a ladder. I climb it and finish up on the roof of this workshop. I pull the ladder up. I see other comrades on the roof of a building next to the one we'd gone into.

Meanwhile the Carabinieri had managed to break down the street door and were going into all the apartments. From my roof I saw them come out onto the balconies, I saw them in the stairways climbing with their helmets and guns, and after a while I saw them come out onto the balconies of the other apartments looking for us. They were waking people in their beds and checking. We stayed there for a bit, we couldn't tell whether the Carabinieri had gone away or not. Then some women from the apartment who'd seen us gave us the sign that they'd gone, they called us to come down. It was almost dawn, the sun was coming up. We were exhausted, worn out. That was enough now. We climbed down and went back home.

Afterword **Nanni Balestrini**

We Want Everything was meant to be the story of the mass worker in Italy, a story that took place at the end of the '60s of last century, already an old story. It is presented as a novel, not so much as an invention of the imagination but as a forced operation to typify the behaviour of an entire social stratum in one person's experiences, creating a collective character who would personify the protagonist of the great wave of struggles of those years, in whom a new political figure appeared on the stage, with new characteristics, new aims, imposing new forms of struggle. He is the Southern proletarian adept at a thousand trades because he has no trade, without a single professional quality even when he possesses a diploma, lacking a steady job and often unemployed or forced into casual service, who can't find work in the South and so seeks it in Turin, in Milan, in Switzerland, in Germany, anywhere in Europe. Who finds the hardest, most exhausting, most inhuman jobs, those that no one else is prepared to do. And who brought about the postwar economic development of Italy and Europe: from Fiat to Volkswagen to Renault, from the mines of Belgium to the Ruhr.

The mass worker has no relation to the old communist tradition, with the channels of organisation of the party and the union. The Italian Communist Party was born in Turin in the wake of the October Revolution, and the factory council movement was born out of the experiences of the workers soviets. Their basis was the skilled worker, highly specialised, who demanded power and wealth because of his technical ability, because of his capacity to create wealth. The vanguard of that movement were the workers' councils established during the factory occupations, who tried to take the place of the owners' managers. The capitalist response of the years that followed made use of various means: Fascism, the economic crisis of 1929, a technological leap (the assembly line and Taylorism), and brought about the defeat of the traditional worker and his substitution with a new type of worker, unskilled, not specialised, mobile, interchangeable, who had a quite different relationship with the machine and the factory.

The main characteristic of this new social figure is above all his ideological estrangement from work and from any professional ethic, the inability to present himself as the bearer of a trade and to identify himself in it. His single obsession is the search for a source of income to be able to consume and survive. Also apparent is his total estrangement from any prospect of development, from any request to participate. For him work and development are understood solely as money, immediately transformable into goods to consume. But little by little as he follows the different stages of the organisation of work (mobility, the factory, unemployment) the estrangement is transformed into a newly discovered political opposition, into the refusal of dependent work and finally in practice into destructive revolt. His individual story becomes the collective story of the working class.

At Fiat in 1969, and then all over Italy, the domination of capital over this figure of the worker was shattered. Not in the formation of a new class consciousness, with the birth of a new ideology, but directly in material demands. It was shattered in the materiality of the struggles, which had different characteristics from those that came before, because they are struggles that are born inside development. The labour-power of the South, which capital wanted to make use of to promote development, unexpectedly revealed an irresolvable contradiction in its contentious behaviour based on material needs. And the worker from the Meridione, ignorant and boorish, plunged the capitalist strategy of the previous 50 years, the mode of production in factories based on the assembly line and the mass worker, into crisis. A complex and tried strategy that had borne fruit and on which the workers' movement, the Communist Party and the unions had built their strategy. And they were plunged into crisis at the same time.

To escape this crisis, which in the course of the 1970s threatened to bring the whole country to a standstill, thanks to the entanglement of the workers' struggle with that of the students and of civil society, the capitalist response made use of tools analogous to those used half a century earlier. In the first place, violent repression entrusted to the police and the judiciary, with the arrest and sentencing of thousands in the workers' vanguard. At the same time, waves of redundancies, taking advantage of the oil shock of 1973. And finally the technological leap, with the disappearance of the assembly line and the robotisation of the factory, which revolutionises the composition of the worker. Apart from a restricted elite of specialised technicians, labour becomes further deskilled and diminished. The flexible worker is born, casualised, without entitlements (holidays, sick leave, pensions, redundancy provisions), hired for a fixed period or part-time, often off the books, generally by those small firms that now do most of the actual work for bigger corporations. The technological investment is amply compensated for by the drastic reduction in personnel, to whom the costs and obligations of a salaried employee do not apply, and by their scant ability to organise in the factory.

This restructuring, thanks to the globalisation of markets, is accompanied by the transfer of entire productive processes to countries in the third world, with minimum wages and non-existent union protection. But even if all of this allowed capital to achieve positive outcomes in the '90s, the profound economic crisis that is rocking it today seems to show that it was only a temporary relief. Capital only appeared to have won a victory; it has triggered a process that leads unavoidably to a confrontation with the underlying issue, expressed clearly 30 years ago in the struggles of the mass worker with the slogan 'refusal of work'. It is an epochal question, that of the end of dependent labour, the form of coerced labour that for a little more than two centuries allowed the birth and growth of industrial civilisation in the west.

More and more the automation of production, and also the possibility in general of trusting almost every type of work and activity to machines and computers, requires a laughably small quantity of human labour power. Therefore why shouldn't everyone profit from the wealth produced by machines and from the time freed from labour? Today, absurdly, work that is no longer necessary continues to be imposed because only through this is it possible to conceive of the distribution of money, allowing the continuation of the cycle of production and consumption and the accumulation of capital.

But it is already a cycle that is slowing; overproduction and the collapse of consumption due to the spread of unemployment and poverty are driving an irreversible crisis, which capitalism frantically tries to save itself from with criminal games of financial speculation. The prospect of the destruction of whole generations, of whole countries, of the planet itself because of the senseless exploitation of its resources—this is the spectacle in which we are assisting today, the spectacle of a perverse voracity to concentrate immense wealth in the hands of just a few and to leave in its wake poverty and the wreckage of a world that could be rich and happy.

But a new era is waiting for humanity, when it will be freed from the blackmail and the suffering of a forced labour that is already unnecessary and the enslavement to money, which prevent the free conduct of activity according to the aptitudes and desires of each and steal and degrade from the rhythm of life, at the same time that there is the real possibility of widespread and general wellbeing. This was the meaning, and could again be the meaning today and in the future, of that old rallying cry: *Vogliamo tutto!*

2013

Notes

1. *Cassa del Mezzogiorno* A government program established in 1950 to stimulate economic development in southern Italy, mainly by the construction of infrastructure such as bridges, dams, roads and irrigation projects. It also provided tax advantages and credit subsidies to encourage investment. Historians say that up to a third of the money was squandered, and many of the fund's beneficiaries were large northern companies given subsidies to build automated factories that employed relatively few workers.

2. *Mirafiori* FIAT's headquarters in Torino, still the largest factory in Italy. The 2-million-square-metre plant employed more than 50,000 workers at its height.

3. *Battipaglia* A town near Salerno in Campania. In 1969 two people were killed during an uprising by almost half the town's population against plans to close the local tobacco and sugar plants.

4. *Reggio* A general strike in Reggio Calabria in July 1970 over the decision to make Catanzaro the regional capital lead to five days of street violence. The government sent 5,000 armed police and carabinieri. Blockades of road and rail links to the city continued for several months, causing considerable economic disruption in the south. Reggio's port was blocked, leaving ships idle in the Straits of Messina, and Italy's main north-south autostrada was cut. The uprising, largely condemned by the left, was taken over by activists from the neofascist MSI, and was put down in February 1971.

5. *Raccomandazione* A word by the right person in someone's ear was often the only way to secure a job in Italy, regardless of qualifications. It continues to be a problem.

6. *Camera del lavoro* The equivalent of Trades Hall, a regional centre for the unions.

7. *Poveri ma belli* Dino Risi's 1957 film *A Girl in a Bikini*

8. *Quartiere Zingone* A small industrial community on the outskirts of Milan built by a financier, Renzo Zingone, in the 1960s.

9. *Lucania* The old Italian name for Basilicata, parts of Calabria and parts of Puglia.

10. *Motta Buondí* A type of packaged sweet snack.

11. *AVIS* Associazione Voluntari Italiani Sangue, Italy's blood bank.

12. *Qualunquista* Someone who is politically apathetic; not interested in politics; also someone driven by self-interest, an individualist.

13. *Me stai cacando 'o cazzo* You're giving me the shits (literally, "You're shitting on my dick")
14. *MALF* La mutua aziendale Fiat, Fiat's health plan.
15. *INAM* l'Istituto nazionale per l'assicurazione contro le malattie, Italy's national health insurance scheme.
16. *Via Roma* One of Turin's main streets.
17. *Potere operaio* 'Workers power'; a number of the groups active around Fiat at that time used this name.
18. *Gigi Riva* Riva, a footballer who played from 1961 to 1976, is still the Italian national team's leading goal scorer. He captained Cagliari to its only Serie A championship in 1969–70 — they were the first team from south of Rome to win.
19. *Avola* In December 1968, landless labourers in the town of Avola, Sicily demonstrated for similar pay and conditions to labourers in nearby Lentini. Police opened fire on a roadblock the labourers had set up outside the town, killing two demonstrators and wounding four.
20. *Unione* l'Unione Communisti Italiani, a maoist political group founded in Rome in 1968 and dissolved in 1978.
21. *Lotta Continua* After the successes of the summer, the name Lotta Continua was adopted by part of the assembly for their project to establish an Italy-wide extraparliamentary revolutionary leftist group.
22. *Unione Industriale* The employer and industry association.
23. *PSIUP* Partito Socialista Italiano di Unitá Proletaria The left-wing PSIUP splintered from the Italian Socialist Party (PSI) after the PSI entered the Moro coalition government in 1963. About one third of the PSI's left wing joined the PSIUP, as well as a large number of activists from left-wing trade unions.
24. *Action squads* A reference to the *squadre d'azione*, paramilitary gangs active during the Fascist era.
25. *Cinesi* Chinese, used as shorthand in the Italian media to describe the new generation of revolutionaries who were opposed to the official left parties and unions.
26. *Bersaglieri* Literally 'marksmen', mobile light-infantry units of the Italian army known for jogging rather than marching on parade.